De Niro's Game

De Niro's Game

Rawi Hage

W F HOWES LTD

This large print edition published in 2009 by
W F Howes Ltd
Unit 4, Rearsby Business Park, Gaddesby Lane,
Rearsby, Leicester LE7 4YH

1 3 5 7 9 10 8 6 4 2

First published in the United Kingdom in 2007
by Old Street Publishing Ltd

A CIP catalogue record for this book is available
from the British Library

ISBN 978 1 40743 426 1

Typeset by Palimpsest Book Production Limited,
Grangemouth, Stirlingshire
Printed and bound in Great Britain
by MPG Books Ltd, Bodmin, Cornwall

For my parents.

'And the breadth *shall be* ten thousand.'
—THE BOOK OF THE PROPHET EZEKIEL

'How, from a fire that never sinks or sets,
would you escape?'
—HERACLITUS

'Moi, j'ai les mains sales. Jusqu'aux coudes.
Je les ai plongées dans la merde et dans le sang.'
—JEAN-PAUL SARTRE

CONTENTS

PART I

ROMA

CHAPTER 1

Ten thousand bombs had landed, and I was waiting for George.

Ten thousand bombs had landed on Beirut, that crowded city, and I was lying on a blue sofa covered with white sheets to protect it from dust and dirty feet.

It is time to leave, I was thinking to myself.

My mother's radio was on. It had been on since the start of the war, a radio with Rayovac batteries that lasted ten thousand years. My mother's radio was wrapped in a cheap, green plastic cover, with holes in it, smudged with the residue of her cooking fingers and dust that penetrated its knobs, cinched against its edges. Nothing ever stopped those melancholic Fairuz songs that came out of it.

I was not escaping the war; I was running away from Fairuz, the notorious singer.

Summer and the heat had arrived; the land was burning under a close sun that cooked our flat and its roof. Down below our white window, Christian cats walked the narrow streets nonchalantly, never crossing themselves or kneeling for

3

black-dressed priests. Cars were parked on both sides of the street, cars that climbed sidewalks, obstructed the passage of worn-out, suffocating pedestrians whose feet, tired feet, and faces, long faces, cursed and blamed America with every little step and every twitch of their miserable lives.

Heat descended, bombs landed, and thugs jumped the long lines for bread, stole the food of the weak, bullied the baker and caressed his daughter. Thugs never waited in lines.

George honked.

His motorcycle's cadaverous black fumes reached my window, and its bubbly noise entered my room. I went downstairs and cursed Fairuz on the way out: *That whining singer who makes my life a morbid hell.*

My mother came down from the roof with two buckets in her hands; she was stealing water from the neighbour's reservoir.

There is no water, she said to me. It only comes two hours a day.

She mentioned something about food, as usual, but I waved and ran down the stairs.

I climbed onto George's motorbike and sat behind him, and we drove down the main streets where bombs fell, where Saudi diplomats had once picked up French prostitutes, where ancient Greeks had danced, Romans had invaded, Persians had sharpened their swords, Mamluks had stolen the villagers' food, crusaders had eaten human flesh, and Turks had enslaved my grand-mother.

War is for thugs. Motorcycles are also for thugs, and for long-haired teenagers like us, with guns under our bellies, and stolen gas in our tanks, and no particular place to go.

We stopped at the city's shoreling, on the ramp of a bridge, and George said to me, I have a *mashkal* (problem).

Talk, I said.

This man, Chafiq Al-Azrak I think his name is, parks his car down from my Aunt Nabila's place. When he leaves, he still reserves the space for himself. I moved the two poles marking his spot so my aunt can park. So she parks, and we go up to have coffee at her place. This Chafiq fellow knocks at my aunt's door and asks her to move her car. It is his space, he says. My aunt says, It is a public space . . . He insults her . . . She shouts . . . I pull out my gun, put it in his face, and kick him out of the house. He runs down the stairs and threatens me from below. But we will show him, won't we, quiet man?

I listened and nodded. Then we hopped back on the motorbike and drove under falling bullets, oblivious. We drove through the noise of military chants and a thousand radio stations all claiming victory. We stared at the short skirts of female warriors and drove beside schoolgirls' thighs. We were aimless, beggars and thieves, horny Arabs with curly hair and open shirts and

Marlboro packs rolled in our sleeves, dropouts, ruthless nihilists with guns, bad breath, and long American jeans.

I will see you tonight, late, George said to me when he dropped me back home. Then he drove away.

Midnight came; the noise of George's motorbike filled the neighbourhood. I went down to the alley where the men watched the late-Friday-night Egyptian movie, smoking on small balconies, gulping cold beer and *araq*, cracking fresh green almonds, and with their filthy yellow nails crushing American cigarettes in folkloric ashtrays. Inside their houses, the impoverished women carefully, economically, dripped water from red plastic buckets over their brown skins in ancient Turkish bathtubs, washing away the dust, the smells, the baklava-thin crust, the vicious morning gossip over tiny coffee cups, the poverty of their husbands, the sweat under their unshaven armpits. They washed like meticulous Christian cats that lick their paws under small European car engines that leak corporate oil extracted by exploited Nigerian workers from underneath the earth where devils roam, and worms gnaw on the roots of dead trees that are suffocated by factory fumes and the greedy breath of white-skinned engineers. Those lazy cats lingered under unwashed cars, watching the passing of Italian shoes, painted nails, colourful and torn-out cuffs, pointy high

6

heels, plastic flippers, stomping naked feet, and delicious exposed ankles that thick hands would bind, release, and slip higher to reach a flow of warm fluid that carefully, generously turned into a modest flood smelling of eel, red fish, and rosewater.

We drove fast toward George's aunt's house. When we arrived, George said, That is Chafiq Al-Azrak's car. He pulled out his gun. I gave the motorcycle gas and made it roar. George shot the wheels of the car, and the air in them was released. He aimed higher and shot the car's lights, the door, the tinted glass, the seat inside, his own reflection in the mirror. He fired silently, and calmly danced around the car, then pointed and fired again. The broken metal was penetrated with tiny, damaging holes, quick and sharp. It was a lethal, entertaining act of vengeance, and I liked it.

When it was over, we fled the scene. I drove the motorcycle through sleepy neighbourhoods with endless wooden doors, and I felt George's gun brushing against my back. We reached the open road, and our cotton shirts welcomed the wind; it molested our skin and dwelt in our ears. I drove fast, impetuously, and the wind stroked my eyes, entered my nostrils and my lungs. I drove through streets of broken lamps, walls covered with bullet holes, spilled blood that turned into dark stains on dusty, neglected sidewalks. I drove and felt thirst in my veins, convalescence and fresh wind in my chest. George was breathing heavily behind my shoulder, like a mad dog, howling to the air in triumph and demonic laughter.

Cocktail, he shouted in my ear. Let's have a cocktail! I made a quick and sharp turn. Like a Mongol rider I swung George's machine to the road, and the back wheel rolled and crushed tiny pebbles. A grey cloud rose from the earth, and I swung around and drove straight to the juice bar that was open all night over the highway on the other side of town, in the Armenian district, far from the Turks who had enslaved my grandmother. We passed Cinema Lucy, where young men and chronic masturbators watched a large screen that showed American women with large chests getting hastily fucked by men with large cocks who were dressed in cowboy suits or as schoolteachers with Afros and 1970s hairdos, over a jazzy tune, on the border of a fancy pool, with maids in white aprons who left their tiny skirts backstage on the director's door or the cameraman's car seat, and bounced their liberated 1970s asses on the edges of long, plastic chairs, ready to serve red cocktails with midget paper umbrellas.

At the juice bar, George and I drank mango topped with white cheese, honey, and nuts.

We sat and sipped our cocktails, licked our fingers, and talked about the gun, and how silent it was.

CHAPTER 2

Ten thousand bombs had split the winds, and my mother was still in the kitchen smoking her long, white cigarettes. She was dressed in black from head to toe, mourning her father and mine. She boiled water on her gas stove, she cut meat on her meat board, and she puffed tobacco against our shattered wall and through our broken glass window. Here, in her kitchen, a bomb had landed and made a wide-open hole in the wall, giving us a splendid view of the vast sky. We wouldn't fix it until winter, until the rain fell and washed away the soil above all the corpses we'd buried. Here in that kitchen my father had died; hers had died farther north.

When George paid his aunt a visit the next day, her car was parked in Chafiq Al-Azrak's space.

Chafiq Al-Azrak came this morning, apologized, and offered to share the space, George's aunt said, and played with her red-dyed hair. Aunt Nabila was in her mid-forties. She worked in a bank. Never married, flirtatious and voluptuous, she dressed in tight skirts, high heels, colourful makeup, and low-cut blouses that showed her generous cleavage jutting forward. She called George 'Gargourty,' a nickname from childhood that made him feel uncomfortable.

I often passed by Aunt Nabila's place looking for George. And she often opened her door in her nightgown, with a cigarette balanced on her round lips. I fantasized about her inviting me in for a coffee, offering me water at the kitchen table, kneeling in worship under my belly button, undoing my Japanese-made zipper, nipping at my secreted fluid, and sweetly, in her little coquettish voice, assuring me that George was not here.

Isn't he at work? she would say. Gargourty is at work!

George, my childhood friend, worked in a poker-machine joint. He cashed money from gamblers who lingered all day on machines that flicked green light on small screens. They pressed buttons and lost their wives' jewels, their fathers' houses and olive trees, their kids' clothes. Everything they owned was sucked in, everything was extracted from their polyester pockets by aces and laughing jokers. George took their money and transferred the credit into their machines, sold them whisky and cigarettes, cleaned the bathroom, opened the door, lowered the air conditioning, swept the dust away, emptied the ashtrays, protected the place, and when the militiamen came he put the money in sealed bags, handed it to them, took his motorbike, and went home.

There must be a way to get a cut, he once said to me when I visited him. Are you in?

Abou-Nahra will cut our heads off if we are caught stealing.

Yeah, it's risky, but there must be a way.

We will be fucking with the militia, I said.

George shrugged his shoulders, inhaled oily black hash, closed his eyes, and held the smoke in his thin chest. Then, slowly, with his eyes closed, he released his breath, extended his arm like a half crucifix, stretched his two fingers, and passed the hash on.

Bombs were falling like monsoon rain in distant India. I was desperate and restless, in need of a better job and money. I worked at the port, where I drove the winch. We emptied weapons from ships. The weapons were stamped with Hebrew, English, and Arabic serial numbers. Some shipments had oil, and we had to hook them up to pipes in trucks. Fruit came from Turkey. Seasick sheep with dripping noses and frightened sounds came also from Turkey. We emptied it all. When the shipments contained weapons, militia jeeps surrounded the whole area. The unloading was always done at night and no light was allowed, not even a cigarette. After a night shift I would go home and sleep through the day. My mother cooked and complained. The few jobs I got at the port were not enough for cigarettes, a nagging mother, and food. Where to go, who to rob, con, beg, seduce, strip, and touch? I was sitting in my room, looking at a wall filled with foreign images, fading posters of teenage singers, blondes with shiny white teeth, Italian football players. I thought, Roma must be a good place to walk freely. The pigeons in the squares look happy and well fed.

I thought about George's proposal and the poker machines. I decided to pay him a visit at his work.

I walked through the little alleys on the way to the casino, passing by Um-Sami, the seamstress whose husband had abandoned her for an Egyptian maid. She was sticking needles into the white gown of a young bride whose wedding would take place in a small chapel with an electronic recording of pitiful bells scratching like an old 1930s record, and whose father had accepted a middle-aged Canadian engineer for a son-in-law, and whose mother was busy making dough and gathering chairs and cutting parsley for the big day, and whose brother was planning to fire his gun in the air in celebration of his sister's official deflowering, and whose cousin would drive her, in his long, polished car, to the church and then to the ship on the Mediterranean Sea. The sea that is filled with pharaoh tears, pirate ship wreckage, slave bones, flowing rivers of sewage, and French tampons.

Across the street from the seamstress, Abou-Dolly the grocer was fanning and driving the flies away from his face and into his rotten vegetables. Abou-Afif was playing backgammon with his nephew Antoine. Claude was still hunting for a husband. It won't be me, I said. It won't be me! The sky was a deep blue. From it, bullets and bombs fell randomly. To look at the sky over our land was to see death diving at you – you, a pool of water on a curved street, a salty sea with red fish, a string bed for boys to jump on; you, embroidered underwear for painted toes to step into, a diamond cover for an arched dagger; you . . .

I was passing by Nabila's place and decided to stop in and see her. She opened the door. I smiled and stood still, without a word, just breathing.

Looking for your friend again? she asked me.

We are all friends here, I replied.

She smiled, laughed, shook her head, and invited me in.

I sat agitated, like a schoolboy who is about to jerk off.

Do you want some coffee?

Yes, I said and looked at her see-through dress. Her thighs were full and round. The lines of her underwear were showing, defining the borders between her majestic ass and the tops of her legs.

She went to the kitchen. I followed her.

I am going to see George, I said.

At work?

Yes.

So why did you come here if you know he is at work?

I thought you might want to send him something, like a sandwich or an apple.

She approached me, pinched my left cheek and said, You are not so innocent, young man, visiting your best friend's aunt while he is at work.

I held her hand; she tried to pull it away. I hung on to her little finger and pulled her over slowly. She smiled. I kissed her neck. She smelled of beauty cream, milk, and fat bankers' cigars. She let me wander my lips over her neck, then laid her open palm on my chest and gently pushed me away.

The coffee is foaming on the stove, and you have to go, young man.

George was waiting for me. I walked toward him and handed him fifty liras. Pretend not to know me, I whispered.

Which machine do you want it in?

What do you mean? I asked.

Which machine? He sounded irritated. I will transfer the amount to that machine.

Oh yes. Number three.

I went to number three and there were fifty liras in credit waiting for me on the upper right-hand corner of the screen.

I played for twenty liras and lost. I went back to him and said that I needed the balance back, the thirty that was left.

He gave it to me.

I walked back to my home, thinking that, yes, there had to be a way.

Ten thousand bombs had dropped like marbles on the kitchen floor and my mother was still cooking. My father was still buried underground; only Christ had risen from the dead, so they say. I was no longer expecting my father to show up at the door, quietly, calmly walking into the kitchen, sitting at that table, waiting for my mother to serve him salad and thin bread. The dead do not come back.

Ten thousand bombs had made my ears whistle, but I still refused to go down to the shelter.

I have lost too many loved ones, my mother said to me. Come down to the shelter.

I did not go.

Ten thousand cigarettes had touched my lips, and a million sips of Turkish coffee had poured down my red throat. I was thinking of Nabila, of poker machines and of Roma. I was thinking of leaving this place. I lit the last candle, drank from the water bucket, opened the fridge, and closed it again. It was empty and melting from the inside. The kitchen was quiet; my mother's radio was far away, buried down in the shelter, entertaining rats and crowded families. When the bombs fell, the shelter became a house, a candy castle and a camp for children to play in, a shrine, a kitchen and a café, a dark, cozy little place with a stove, foam mattresses, and games. But it was stuffy, and I'd rather die in the open air.

A bomb fell in the next alley. I heard screams; a river of blood must be flowing by now. I waited; the rule was to wait for the second bomb. Bombs landed in twos, like Midwestern American tourists in Paris. The second bomb fell. I walked slowly out of the apartment. I walked down the stairs and through the back alleys, guided by screams and the smell of powder and scattered stones. I found the blood beside a little girl. Tony the gambler was already there, with his car ready to go. He was half-naked and stuttering, M-a-r-y mother of God, Mary m-o-t-h-e-r of God. He kept repeating this with difficulty, breathless and frozen. I carried the little girl. Her wailing mother was hysterical; she followed me to the back seat of the car. I took off my shirt and wrapped it around the girl's bleeding ribs. Tony flew his car toward the hospital. He honked his siren. The streets were empty; the buildings looked hazy and unfamiliar. The girl's blood dripped on my finger, down my thighs. I was bathing in blood. Blood is darker than red, smoother than silk; on your hand it is warm like warm water and soap. My shirt was turning a royal purple. I shouted and called the little girl by her name, but my shirt was sucking up her blood; I could have squeezed it and filled the Red Sea and plunged my body in it, claimed it, walked its shore and sat in its sun. My hands were pressing on the little girl's open wound. She faded away; her pupils rolled over and disappeared into a white, soft, dreamy pillow. Her head was leaning toward her mother's round breast. Her mother picked up Tony's mantra and they both repeated, Mary mother of God, Mary mother of God. The little girl was leaving to go to Roma, I thought. She is going to Roma, lucky girl. Tony honked a farewell in a sad rhythm to the empty streets.

The next morning I was meeting George down at the corner by Chahine the butcher's. There was a line of women waiting for the meat. Inside, goats were hung, stripped of their skin. White and red meat fell from above, pieces were cut, crushed, banged, cut again, ground, put in paper bags, and handed to the women in line, women in black, with melodramatic, oil-painted faces, in churchgoer submissive positions, in Halloween horrors, in cannibal hunger for crucifix flesh, in menstrual cramps of virgin saints, in castrated hermetic positions, on their knees and at the mercy of knives and illiterate butchers. Red-headed flies strolled everywhere, there was animal blood on the floor, butchers' knives paraded on stained yellow walls. The bombing had stopped, and women had come out from their holes to gather tender meat for their unemployed husbands to sink their nicotine-stained teeth into and seal their inflated bellies.

George was walking down the street toward me.

When I spotted him, he waved to me. A man in a green militia suit stopped him. They shook hands; George gave him three kisses on the cheek.

As I waited, I watched the flies resting on the mosaic tiles, feasting on perfect round drops of blood.

Who is that? I asked George.

Khalil. He works with Abou-Nahra.

Maybe it is not a good thing that he sees us together, I said, thinking of the poker machines.

He hardly ever comes to the casino. Not to worry.

Maybe there is a way to get a cut of the money, I said. And it might be simple. I come and pay you the money, and you press the credit in the machine while I am playing. Does the machine keep records . . . I mean, if you have a straight flush, for instance, would it record the winning strike somewhere?

No. I don't think so, George said.

We have to be sure. I will pass by on Monday. We can try it. While I am playing, inject some credit in there. A small amount, not much, just to try.

Come by in the morning, early . . . usually there is no one there, George said.

And maybe we should stop meeting in the open for now, I said.

I went to the little girl's funeral, the little girl who was on her way to Roma. Her mother was wailing.

Women with veils over their hair filled the little alley. My mother went to the funeral too. They come to our funerals, we go to theirs, she whispered to me in a moral tone.

The girl's father flew back from Saudi Arabia, where he worked in the burning fields of sand and oil. He walked to the front, crossing his thick hands, his sunburned face in flames, his dark eyes sobbing, his feet dragging on dust and sand. The small white coffin was carried by the girl's cousins and neighbours on the long walk to the cemetery; as the sunlight landed on the white wooden box it twinkled, the wood and the metal twinkled, everyone twinkled, even I twinkled. Men in grey suits and black ties moved slowly, past the closed stores, and sagged their heavy heads toward the floor. Tony was behind me, stuttering and telling his tale of driving, death, and hospitals. I was surrounded by familiar faces filled with grief. Behind us, the mother was fainting, hanging on to the women's arms. She was pulled forward, slapped and sprinkled with rosewater by women who were beating their chests, chanting farewell and wedding songs, wailing, waving white handkerchiefs high in the air toward the Leaning Tower of Pisa.

CHAPTER 3

Monday morning, I walked to George's work. No one was there but him. I paid; while I played, he injected credit into the poker machine. Success! I collected and left.

I met George that evening, on the stairs of the church.

Let's wait and see if they notice, I told him. Maybe they have a way of finding out. It is not too big an amount. If they find out, we could pass it off as a mistake.

I gave him half of the money, and we separated.

On my way home, I went by Nabila's place. There was no light on at her house. The city was dark. No TV was on, no water was cold; ice cream melted in cube-shaped fridges and the old men drank whiskies with no ice. I saw Rana, our neighbour, and hardly recognized her at first. She said, *Bonsoir*, and I replied, *Bonsoirayn* for you, and where are you going in the dark with a silk shawl on your shoulders?

To the store to buy candles.

With a face like yours, who needs candles? I said.

Rana laughed and told me to go home and to be careful not to trip on the stairs. It is dark, she said.

There is a moon close by, I said.

It is still dark.

We can light a candle, I said.

Where? she asked. Your mother's place or mine? And she put her hands on her curved hips. Her hair fell onto her shoulders, and her wide black eyes waited for my response.

In Roma, I said.

What?

I did not answer and crossed to the other side of the street.

Saad, our neighbour, got a visa to Sweden.

He threw a party the night before his departure. He knocked at our door and invited me to the goodbye celebration.

Stockholm, he said. Yeah, Stockholm, and shook his head.

At seven that night, I showed up at his place, hungry. His mother had prepared a *mazah*. I broke the bread and dipped my fingers in small, round brown plates. The electricity was still cut off, but there were candles and a lantern lit up. Some flies had travelled over from the butcher store, and they hovered around the lanterns then burned. Saad's brother Chahker – a pompous idiot, if you ask me – was there. So were his cousin Miriam and his mother and father and a few of his relatives and friends. George was there, too, drinking and smoking quietly.

I looked at George and he smiled at me.

Jokes were made about Sweden and Swedish women, blondes and the cold weather. A man with thick villager's hands and a rough neck and a mountain accent started to sing. Saad's family joined in. They sang songs that were foreign to me, villagers' songs that I had never heard before, hymns of goodbye and return and marriage, warnings not to marry foreign women: Our women are the best in the world, they do not dishonour you, and our land is the greenest. Go make money and come back . . . She will wait for you.

But those who leave never come back, I sang in my heart.

George drank heavily. He laughed and flirted with Saad's cousin. It made Chahker nervous and jealous. Chahker had asked for the hand of Saad's cousin, but she had refused. She was young, with red cheeks and long legs. She was caught between her villager's norms and trying hard to show off her newly acquired urban manners. Saad and his family were refugees from a small town; they had fled when a gang of armed forces attacked and massacred a great number of villagers and farmers.

By late that evening, George was very drunk. I pulled him down to the street and he threw up on the kerb.

He reached for his motorbike, but I stopped him, and he swung punches at me. I held his hands, talked to him, trying to calm him down, asking him not to shout. Then I dragged him to his aunt's place. I left him lying at the bottom of the stairs, ran up and knocked at Nabila's door. She opened the door, frantic. Who? she said. Is Gargourty okay? Who? Oh, Virgin Mary, help us. Who?

No one, I said. Everyone is alive. George is just drunk and sick.

Where is he?

Downstairs.

Nabila ran down the stairs, her hand barely touching the ramp, half-naked and filled with fear; she caressed George's cheeks and kissed the tips of his fingers.

Together, we picked him up and carried him upstairs. Nabila cleaned him, took off his shirt, his shoes, and his pants, and gave him her own bed and covered him with an old blanket. Then she sat on the sofa and wept.

I worry about him, you know? When a phone rings late at night I often think that someone is dead. He has a gun. Why does he carry a gun?

It is his work. He needs it, I said.

He should go to school. I will pay for his studies. Let him go back to school.

She offered me coffee, and I accepted. She tiptoed to the kitchen and poured water in a *rakwah*, grabbed a small spoon, the coffee, the sugar. She boiled the coffee thrice, brought it on a tin tray, and let it rest like a gracious wine before pouring it for me in a small cup.

I drank. Nabila watched.

Is it sweet enough for you? she asked.

Yes.

I read George's cup the other day. It was dark, so dark. Let me read yours.

I do not believe, I whispered.

She held my cup and looked inside. She saw waves, a distant land, a woman, and three signs.

The usual superstitious beliefs, I said.

No! I see it. Come over here, see? This is the road, this is the sea, and this is the woman. You see?

No, but . . .

She smelled like the night. I slipped my hand onto her knee.

Nabila held my hand, pressed it, and moved it toward my chest. No, Bassam, go home. She kissed my hand as if I were her own child. Take care of George, tell him to go back to school. You should go back to school too. You are a smart kid, you like to read. As a child you recited poems with your uncle.

Goodnight, I said.

You take care of Gargourty, Nabila said, and followed me to the door.

I went home to my bed. When I woke up, Saad had gone to Sweden.

★　　★　　★

24

Bombs fell, warriors fought, people ate, and the garbage piled up on the corners of our streets. Cats and dogs were feasting and getting fatter. The rich were leaving for France and letting their dogs roam loose on the streets: orphan dogs, expensive dogs, potty-trained dogs, dogs with French names and red bowties, fluffy dogs, well-bred dogs, china dogs, genetically modified dogs, and incestuous dogs that clung to one another in packs, covered the streets in tens, and gathered under the command of a charismatic three-legged mutt. The most expensive pack of wild dogs roamed Beirut and the earth, and howled to the big moon, and ate from mountains of garbage on the corners of our streets.

I walked past hills of garbage. The smell of bones, the sight of all that is rotten and refused, made me rush down, aimless, toward the gas station, where I saw long lines of cars waiting to fill their tanks. I saw Khalil, George's friend, in a militia jeep with no roof and no windows. He drove straight into a crowded gas station. He stopped his machine, came down, took his rifle, and shot in the air. He shouted, waved his hands, and ordered cars to go back, forward, and to the side. Then he fired more shots. The cars dispersed. Khalil drove his jeep close to the pumping station, filled his gas tank, and drove away.

That night, I went up to the roof. There were no bombs exploding like colliding stars. I gazed at the calm, obscure sky that settled above me like a murky swamp, hanging upside down. All seemed about to fall, to spread darkness and drown. On the roof was a large water barrel that I usually hid things under. I pulled out a piece of hose, wrapped it around my waist, and waited for George to show up. The moon was round and hovering above my city. We, the moon and I, watched lit candles flickering quietly in young virgins' rooms while they were getting dressed for the night, climbing into their single beds, throwing their combed hair on goose-feather pillows stuffed by grandmothers with names like Jamileh and Georgette, veiling their pubic hair in cotton and silk sheets, dreaming of hairless white men in sports cars and provincial suits telling them fairy tales, in a foreign language, in secret, to make their little toes curl under the covers, away from their mothers' eyes.

My accomplice was the dirty moon. He shone, and I watched.

When George came, we drove to Surssok, an old bourgeois neighbourhood with maids who served rich housewives wearing chic French dresses and possessing walk-in closets filled with leather shoes. They had apartments in Paris, and husbands who imported cigarettes, containers, and car parts, who coughed in Swiss banks at wooden mahogany desks occupied by nephews of chocolate factory owners, grandsons of landlords of African cocoa fields dotted with workers with bruised fingers, who worked under many suns, who worked on Sundays and Fridays. Those husbands ate in velvet restaurants and stayed in expensive hotels with large beds, Portuguese cleaning ladies, and thick towels. They puffed thick Cuban cigars, consulted their round, golden watches, spat filthy words like 'shipments' and 'invoices' over cognac and elevator music, words that bounced off mirrors and bald bartenders with multilingual prostitutes who drooled long, silver earrings on executive suits while looking bored and bitter.

American cars have no locks on the gas tanks, I said to George. They are the good ones to empty.

We stopped next to a white Buick. I pulled the hose from around my waist. I spun it in the air; it whistled. George laughed, and I spun it some more, and it whistled again. I opened the gas tank cover; George laid his motorbike on its side. I drove the hose inside the gas tank; it slipped gently in, like a snake into a ground hole. I lay my lips on its tail, sucked in, inhaled a flow of gas. It rushed toward my teeth. I directed the stream toward our gas tank. We filled the tank, and then we crawled, escaped and evaporated through a night of mist and dew. The smell of gas in my throat made me nauseous. We stopped at a store and got a can of milk. I drank it and vomited bread and poison between two rusty cars.

Thursday morning, I passed by George's work again. I handed him some money, installed myself on a stool facing a poker machine, and played. On the screen I saw my credit increasing. There was an old, unshaven man sitting two machines down from me. A cigarette burned on his lip and made his wrinkled eyelid twitch. He was hitting the buttons almost blindly, without looking.

I tried to imitate his speed, his nonchalant attitude, his familiarity with fate and chance, his indifference to loss, his silence, his equanimity. He hung off his stool as if ropes from above held his defeated body, lifted his arms, and dropped them in suicidal freefalls on round plastic buttons.

That evening, I met George at his place. He lived alone, down beside the French stairs, in an old stone house with little furniture, a photo of his dead mother under a high ceiling, and emptiness. He never mentioned his father. The word was that his father was a Frenchman who had come to our land, planted a seed in his mother's young womb, and flown back north like a migrating bird.

I pulled out the money I'd made that morning, counted half and gave it to him.

We sat in George's living room on an old couch between echoing walls. We whispered conspiracies, exchanged money, drank beer, rolled hash in soft, white paper, and I praised Roma.

Roma? George said. Go to America. Roma, there is no future. Yeah, it is pretty, but America is better.

How about you? I said. Are you going or staying?

I am staying. I like it here.

He put some music on. We sang with it, and drank.

I need to fix the motorbike; the exhaust needs to be changed, George told me. Pass by the casino on Tuesday morning and you can play again. Some more money won't hurt us. And take your time, you looked like you were watching your back last time. Don't worry if Abou-Nahra or someone from the militia comes in. If something's wrong, I will bring you a whisky with no ice. That is the cue for you to leave. *Capice*, Roma man?

We were both high, sleepy, and feeling rich.

That night I slept on George's sofa; he slept on his mother's bed.

I woke up when dawn sprung its shine over my brown eyes, pulled on my eyelid, and asked me to walk.

George was still asleep. His gun was on the table, and the cash was crushed under its weight. No wind will ever move it, I thought. When I walked out, the city was calm. The streets were laden with morning dust and parked cars, and everything was closed except the early baker, Saffy. I bought a *man'oushe* from the baker and ate it. Taxis were not hustling yet, stores had not rolled up their metal doors, women were not boiling their coffee, vegetables were not loaded onto pushing carts, the horses were not running and the gamblers were not betting, fighters were not cleaning their guns. Everyone was asleep. Beirut, the city, was safe for now.

CHAPTER 4

Ten thousand bombs had fallen and I was waiting for death to come and scoop its daily share from a bowl of limbs and blood. I walked down the street under the falling bombs. The streets were empty. I walked above humans hidden in shelters like colonies of rats beneath the soil. I walked past photos of dead young men posted on wooden electric poles, on entrances of buildings, framed in little shrines.

Beirut was the calmest city ever in a war.

I walked in the middle of the street as if I owned it. I walked through the calmest city, an empty city that I liked; all cities should be emptied of men and given to dogs.

A bomb fell not far from me. I looked for the smoke, waited for the moaning and screams, but there were none. Maybe the bomb had hit me. Maybe I was dead in the backseat of a car, my blood pouring out little happy fountains and mopped up by a stranger's clothes. My blood drunk by a warlord or some God whose thirst could never be quenched, a petty tribal God, a jealous God celebrating his tribe's carnage and gore, a God who chooses one servant over the other, a lonely, lunatic, imaginary God, poisoned by lead and silver bowls, distracted by divine orgies and arranged marriages, mixing wine and water and sharpening his sword and handing it down to his many goatskin prophets, his castrated saints, and his conspirator eunuchs.

On an old lady's balcony I saw a bird in a cage, a cat crouched beneath it on the ground, and a hungry dog looking for cadavers to sink his purebred teeth into, looking to snatch a soft arm or a tender leg. Human flesh is not forbidden us dogs, those laws apply only to humans, the unshaven poodle said to me. I nodded and agreed, and walked on some more. I heard rifles and more bombs. This time the bombs were heading toward the Muslim side, to inflict wounds and to make more little girls' blood flow. Bombs that leave are louder than the ones that land.

I stood in the middle of the street and rolled a cigarette. I inhaled, exhaled, and the fumes from my mouth grew like a shield. The bombs that came my way ricocheted off it, and bounded and skipped along the sky to faraway planets.

Night came, as it always does. George and I decided to go to the mountains. We drove up to Broumana, a high village that had been turned into an expensive refuge for the wealthy. Bars and cafés were everywhere, with round tables and fast waiters. Half-naked, painted women walked the narrow village streets, and militiamen drove past them in their Mercedes with crosses hanging off the mirrors. Loud dancing music flowed out of restaurants. We entered a club, sat at a table, and watched couples dancing, people drinking and not talking. No one has anything to say; don't you know that war spreads silence, cuts tongues, and flattens stones? the drink said to me. George and I both smelled of deodorant, silk shirts, fake watches, and foam shaving cream. George pointed at a woman in a blue dress. That one I want, he said. I ordered two glasses of whisky while he smiled at the woman. She turned her face to her girlfriend, then they both looked back our way and giggled. Let's go, George said to me. He stood up and walked toward the women. While he talked to the woman in the blue dress, I stayed at the table. I paid for the drinks and sipped my whisky and watched everyone. George was moving his hands, and leaning his chest against the woman's shoulders. On the dance floor, women were shaking their hips to Arabic songs. A man with a thick moustache put his hand on my shoulder and said, There is nothing in this world, my friend. Nothing is worth it; enjoy yourself. Tomorrow we might all die. Here, *yallah*, cheers. We banged our glasses, and he entered the dance floor waving his arms in the air, an empty glass in his hand, a cigarette on his lower lip.

George came back to our table, leaned on me, and whispered, Why didn't you follow me?

Her friend is alone, and they asked about you, in French, my love, in French! I got her number. Is that my drink? You should have come. They are rich and they are leaving now. If only we had a car we could have driven them back to my place.

I drank, and George went onto the floor and danced alone. He drank a great deal while he danced.

Eventually he came back and called the waiter. He pulled bills from his pocket, paid, and drank some more.

Fuck them all. I will fuck them all.

Who? I asked.

God and all the angels and his kingdom, George said.

He was very drunk by then, delirious and violent. He pulled out his gun and shouted, I will fuck them all. I grabbed his hand, pulled it under the table, aimed the gun to the floor, and whispered to him softly, On your mother's grave, I am asking you . . . me, your brother, me, your brother, who will spill blood for you. Give me the gun.

I kissed his cheek, wrapped my arm around his shoulder, and calmed him down. Then I pulled the gun slowly from his hand and hid it against my belly under my most expensive silk shirt. I tried to make him leave, but he resisted. I begged him again. I showered him with sweet talk, praises, and kisses.

We will fuck them all later, I said. Tomorrow, not

to worry, we will fuck their cars, their mirrors, and their round tires. By Allah, Jesus, and his angels, come, let us leave.

We walked outside. George was cursing, pushing people, and shouting on the streets. I have no father, and no mother, and no God, you *ya wlad al-sharmuta* (sons of bitches). I have money, you whores, to pay you all off! He pulled more bills from his pocket and threw them in the air.

I dragged George off the main street and walked to the side street, where little village shacks had turned into cafés and fancy whorehouses with velvet sofas and pink neon signs. I stopped a young man, who was trotting his way toward the music, and asked him to recommend a place for us to stay. The man pointed me to an inn, and we walked in that direction. I left George outside, leaning on the curb, and walked inside the place. I got a room, took George upstairs, and laid him on the bed. He slept.

It was still dark outside, still noisy. Still the neon lights in that village flickered and called the young. I ignored all that temptation and took George's motorcycle and drove toward the city.

The wind kept me awake. I drove like the wind that kept me awake. I drove faster than the wind that kept me awake. I was escaping time and space, like flying bullets. Death does not come to you when you face it; death is full of treachery, a coward who only notices the feeble and strikes the blind. I was flying on the curved road, sliding down rugged mountains, brushing against car lights, forgotten trees, and wildflowers that closed at night. I was a bow with a silver arrow, a god's spear, a travelling merchant, a night thief. I was flying on a mighty machine that shattered winds and rattled the earth underneath me. I was a king.

A young kid at a checkpoint pointed an AK-47 at me. Your papers, he said. I gave him my birth certificate, with my age and the place of my birth and my ancestors' births, and the colour of my eyes, and my religion, and a photo of me smiling to the Armenian photographer, looking at his beloved 4 x 5 camera that his father had brought from Russia and carried through the Syrian Desert while the young Turks slaughtered his cousins on doorsteps, and aimed their rifles on high crosses, killed all the goats, and sang glorious modernity chants.

Who does the bike belong to? asked the kid.

My friend, I said.

Lift your arms.

I did. The kid searched me, and when he touched my gun he put his hand on my throat and grabbed the gun fast. He stepped back and pointed his rifle at me.

Come down off the bike slowly and lie on the floor, he said.

I obeyed.

Who is your friend?

George, nicknamed De Niro, I said.

You have a release paper for the gun?

No.

Wait here, the kid said. Stay on the floor and do not move. I will shoot you if you move a toe. He called his superior. A man in his thirties in a black T-shirt, army shoes, moustache, and a beard walked toward me. He held George's gun in his hand like it was his own.

Is this gun stolen? he asked me, waving his flashlight in my face.

No, I said.

What is your name?

Bassam.

Where do you live?

Achrafieh.

What do you do?

I work at the port.

So you are a thief.

No, I said.

Yeah, you work at the port and steal things, don't you? You are a thief.

We are all thieves in this war, I said.

You are answering back! The man slapped me, then dragged me and pushed me inside his green jeep. He puffed like a hyena as he left, swinging the gun toward the sand on the ground.

Three hours passed, and I was still waiting in the back of the jeep. At dawn, when the night was painted with brightness and slowly erased by the early sun, the little militia boy drove the motorcycle away and disappeared into the hills. The checkpoint was dismantled and I was in the back of a moving jeep, feeling the mountain air and my hunger.

The militiaman in front drove like a madman, as if he was rushing a wounded person to a hospital. The jeep jerked and flew in the air, and my body tossed and bumped against the seats. I clung to the metal bar like a monkey clings to a branch. I swung off the bar, and my feet flew like those of a dancing horse. The militiaman drove the wrong way through narrow one-way streets, forcing cars to retreat in fear. He broke off and the wheels shrieked against the asphalt. My hands slipped off the bar and I flew across the back of the jeep. I moaned in pain. The militiaman got out the jeep, pulled out his gun, aimed high, and shot in the air. The cars in his way started to retreat, honking in panic. He stood in the middle of the street, his legs apart, his gun in the air, his shoulders lowered, his head like a row of bricks fixed in one direction. He lowered his arm, waited, lifted his arm again and shot a few more rounds. When the way was clear, he climbed back in the jeep. He cursed all the Christian saints in one concise sentence and drove us up the hill to a military base.

I was marched into an office. A photo of the highest commander, known as Al-Rayess, hung on the wall. I could see a cedar tree and flag behind it.

Sit down. Now, who is the gun for? the militiaman asked. He walked around me. Where did you get it? And who did you steal the bike from?

George, known as De Niro. He is my friend, he works with Abou-Nahra. He owns the gun and the bike. I did not steal anything.

Abou-Nahra, the commander? the militiaman asked.

Yes.

I will call Abou-Nahra. And why do you have your friend's gun?

He was drunk. I took it from him.

I will check with Abou-Nahra. If you are lying to me, you're going to rot in a cell, understood? What is your friend's name again?

George. If you tell the commander 'De Niro,' he will know who you are talking about.

And what is your nickname? Al Pacino?

My captor led me to an empty room with a foam mattress. I slept, and when I woke up I stared at the concrete walls. The mattress was dotted with cigarettes holes. I pulled a box of cigarettes out of my pocket; it was flattened by the weight of my body. I searched my pocket for matches but couldn't find any. I banged at the door. No one answered. I stuck my ear to the door, but all I heard was a distant radio. I recognized Fairuz lamenting through the corridors.

*   *   *

The next day, De Niro came with an order of release from Abou-Nahra, and I was freed.

George and I drove the motorcycle down the highway. The heat was unbearable. Taxi drivers were waiting in their old Mercedes on the corners of the streets, in the shade of dirty walls. We zoomed through traffic jams. We drove on sidewalks, through alleyways, and in the middle of lanes, across dusty and unpaved roads.

Dust flew onto shop windows, dust landed on silky, exposed thighs; everyone inhaled it, everyone saw through it, dust from the undertaker's shovel, dust of demolition, dust of fallen walls, dust falling from Christian foreheads on a holy Thursday. Dust was friendly and loved us all. Dust was Beirut's companion.

Let's eat, I said to George.

Man'oushe or *kunafah*? he asked.

Kunafah, I said.

We stopped at a store with a screen door and we sat at a round table. The mirror on the wall above us was stained and barely gave off a reflection. The worker behind the counter had a large moustache and wielded several knives. I drank water. George lit a cigarette. A woman with a baby in her arms walked in. The news was on: two were dead, five injured; an Arab diplomat was visiting Beirut; an American diplomat was also visiting Beirut. The moon was round, and the diplomat's flag was on it, and an extraterrestrial sniper was using it for target practice.

We ate our *kunafah* plates. I watched the baby play and nibble on a plastic gun. I needed a shave and a bath, and we all needed water. I gave back George's gun, under the table. George's cigarette burned in an ashtray; mine was still in George's box. His sad eyes reminded me that his mother was dead, that his father had left, that my father was also dead. I thought about how, after my father's death, my uncle Naeem had visited more often. I had watched him on Sundays, giving money to my mother, and my mother, with her eyes lowered to the floor, took it and shoved it down into her bosom. Naeem took me for long walks, bought me clothes and books. And when I said to him that my father was with God, he said to me that there was no God, that God is man's invention.

I finished my plate; George gave me a cigarette. I thought about my mother, how she would cook all day, complain, and ask my uncle for money. My uncle was a communist. One night, he fled to the West Side. The militia came looking for him. They knocked at my mother's door in the middle of the night and asked for Naeem the communist.

I contemplated the flies barred by the store's door, longing to come in. Only dust flew in and out as it pleased. Beirut is an ancient Roman city,

I thought. There is a city buried under our feet. The Romans also turned to dust. When I opened the door to leave, the flies rushed in.

George drove me back to my mother's home. And I slept above ancient Rome, dreaming, while the city still breathed dust.

CHAPTER 5

Each daybreak, the women of our building gathered over morning coffee. They talked about the price of vegetables, meat, and fruit. They repeated what they'd heard on the news, like colourful parrots on a pirate's deck.

The women's shouting woke me. I washed my face and brushed my teeth, and as I did so, I heard someone calling Rana's name. I put my shorts on and walked to the living room. I greeted the women; in return, they shouted out my name. Salma, our next-door neighbour, asked me for a kiss: Come here and kiss your aunt Salma. No matter how big you get, you're still our baby here.

I kissed her and moved toward Rana. She blushed; the women held their breath; Rana's mother smiled. I looked at Rana and said, What are you doing, hanging out with the old?

The women shouted and jeered at me. No one is old here, young man!

I can shoot my husband and get a younger man any time, Abla said, and everyone laughed.

Rana blushed again. I smiled, and my mother poured coffee with a grin on her face. They all shouted and talked. Rana's cup was being read. She looked breathtaking in her short skirt. Her bosom rose and fell with her breath, her eyes were outlined in dark black lines, and she sat with her legs crossed, protecting her virginity from predactors' eyes, tongues, and crooked teeth.

I left the room and waited on the stairs at the entrance to our building. Soon, Rana came down with her mother. Her mother walked by me first, and I nodded farewell. Rana was trailing behind; I grabbed her by the wrist.

So what did the cup predict for Rana today? I asked.

It says that my hand will be taken.

By whom?

By the one who is leaving.

Sad, I said.

No, not if I leave too.

I will pick you up at six this evening.

I am busy.

Doing what?

Just busy. Bassam, please, you have to let go of my hand now, people are watching.

I opend my palm, and she left.

Abou-Nahra asked me to join his militia, George said to me.

Don't do it, George, I warned him.

He said they need men at the front line.

Say no.

He will give my job to someone else. George poured whisky and looked me in the eye.

44

We have to leave, I said. We have to get organized. Do a big hit and leave. And we have to time it for when there is enough money in the cash to cover a big win. Let me know. I looked him back in the eye.

What is it with you and Rana? he asked.

How do you know about Rana?

Everyone knows everything in this place. She has grown.

I nodded.

You can meet her here. I will give you the key to my place. My mother won't show up, he said. He looked at me and smiled.

We drank. From his balcony we could see the roofs of houses covered with white laundry, TV antennas, and empty water barrels. The houses were all connected by loose electrical wires tied on wooden poles, filling the concrete city that has no trees for Judas to hang from, no meadows for invaders to roam, only flat roofs and mortals waiting their turn for water and bread. On the pavement there were kids' bicycles, and the clay marks of kids' drawings. Inside our houses, there were women stranded in kitchens, cooking. From below a radio was playing, a mother was calling her kid, a few passing cars rolled slowly through our narrow street. There was that silence, that quietness before bombs fall and teeth shatter and kids piss in their older brothers' shorts, and young girls menstruate before their time, and windows shatter, and glass slices our dark flesh wide open.

Johnny Walker is the best whisky, George said to me. Ice or no ice, this is the life, my friend. He lifted his glass and kissed it.

I waited for Rana downstairs, but she didn't show up. I called to Danny, our neighbour Nahla's son, who was riding on his VelAmos bicycle. I said, Come here. Go to the Damouny family, enter their house when no one is looking, and give Rana this letter. No one should see it, you understand? No . . . come here! You understand? No one should see it.

Yes, the little boy nodded.

You will get something good later. Go now, do not be late.

Danny smiled and darted down the stairs and flew like a pigeon toward Rana's house.

Rana and I met down at the French stairs. It was dark, and I saw her coming down the slope, walking between the cars, concealing herself in the walls' shadows.

When she saw me she waved discreetly, from afar.

I held her hand and took her round the back of a building. I leaned against a wall and pulled her toward me.

You have to stop holding my hand like that, Rana protested.

No one is looking.

You have to ask for permission, she said playfully.

From whom?

From me.

Since when?

Since I won that fight and wrestled you to the ground and made you eat dirt. She laughed.

I kissed her on the cheek; I put my arm around her waist.

She gave me back my hand, pushed me away slowly, and said, Not here.

Come, I said.

I held her wrist and led her up the stairs, and in total darkness I found George's door. I searched for the lock, feeling it with my fingers like a blind man on his wedding night, like a lion in the fox's den. I drove the key in and turned my wrist in a smooth, slow twist. I held Rana's hand and pulled her inside George's house. She resisted, but I kissed her neck. I locked the door, searched for a candle to light. When I struck a match and the fire started to dance on the tips of my fingers, she blew on it and said to me, No. No light.

I laid ten thousand kisses on her body, under a cascade of sweet falling bombs. Our clothes were on the floor like carpets for prayers, our bodies on the bed like dancing corpses. I laid another thousand kisses on her and the bombs fell louder and closer. I slipped my hand under her skirt. She held it and resisted me. I snuck my other hand toward her breast. She let me do this, so I pulled down her bra, feeling her nipples: dark, soft, pointy, and motherly. I followed my tongue as it led me to her belly button. She pushed me away then, and said, Stop it. Stop, please, Bassam, stop. My mother must be looking for me. I told her I am going to see Nada. I have to leave.

I will walk with you.

Walk with me? Or run with me?

We ran through the falling bombs. When we arrived at her home, Rana went down the stairs to the shelter, and I walked back above ground.

Abou-Nahra was in his fifties. He had grey hair and a golden tooth. An Arabic-language teacher by trade, he had left teaching to become a high commander in the Christian militia. He was bald and round, always carried a gun on his waist, and the long, thick chain around his neck had a collection of icons and crosses that pressed against his bulky chest hair. He was in charge of the south district of East Beirut, and was credited with setting up a tax system to collect money from houses, gas stations, and stores to support the war. He had also established mini-casinos and poker machines that collected a great deal of money. Abou-Nahra drove a large Range Rover, and two cars always followed his vehicle as protection. In traffic jams, his bodyguards stuck their weapons out of their windows and shot in the air to make way for his highness. Everyone knew Abou-Nahra. Abou-Nahra was into Christianity, money, and power.

George had met him through Aunt Nabila,

whom Abou-Nahra was 'courting' at the time. Nabila asked Abou-Nahra to give her beloved nephew a job, and he did. After Nabila left Abou-Nahra, George's job was in jeopardy.

There is always a price, George said to me. He wants me to join his militia. He sent Khalil the other day to ask me if I want to go with Khalil down to the green line.

What did you say?

I said that I couldn't leave the casino.

Khalil said he would pass by after we closed and we could go for a while, shoot a few bullets, empty a few magazines, see the men, and come back; it wouldn't be long. I waited for him, but he never showed up. He will pass by tomorrow, I am sure of it.

I will come with you, I said. Give him a rendezvous point. Do not go alone; I will come with you. And keep your gun loaded.

Do you think they know about our scheme at the casino?

No, but just in case, keep your gun loaded. If they do know, Abou-Nahra would have given an order for a hit. I will come with you. Just give Khalil a meeting place.

I saw the kid, Danny, playing with marbles on a patch of sand. I called him over and he ran up to me.

Did you give Rana the letter the other day?

Yes, he said.

49

What did she do?

She read it and smiled.

Here. I pulled some change from my pocket. Go buy some more candy for you and your friends. He raced over to his friends and they all ran, jumping up and down, toward Abou-Fouad's store.

Rana was on George's bed. She lay on her belly, lifted her ankles in the air, straightened her toes, and put her hand on my chest.

Do you love me? she asked.

I kissed her on the mouth.

Do you love me? she repeated louder.

Yes, of course, I said and puffed smoke that hushed my words.

She held my chin between her fingers and looked me in the eye. Look at me here, in my eyes, she said. Do you love me?

Yes, I do, I said. I tried to kiss her breast, but she pushed my face back on the pillow and said: I will smash your face if you're lying to me, Bassam Al-Abyad! I know you. You can never fool me. It is me, Rana, remember? I will shoot you, you hear me. My hand on the cross, I will shoot you.

I laughed and held her waist. She remained silent and looked up at the high ceiling. Then she kissed me and fixed her dress, pulled up her bra, and asked me to zip up her dress. I kissed her shoulders, and she left.

★　★　★

George and I met Khalil down near the electric-company building. Khalil was in a jeep in the driver's seat. Another militiaman, nicknamed Abou-Haddid, was sitting in the back seat with a Czech Kalashnikov in his left hand.

George kissed Khalil and introduced me. We chatted a little, found common acquaintances that we knew, talked about cars and guns. Abou-Hadid said that he knew a man called Charbel who worked at the port with me.

George sat next to Khalil in the jeep. I followed them on the motorbike. We crossed empty streets and bomb-shattered buildings and went through a few checkpoints smoothly. Everyone knew Khalil.

When we arrived at the headquarters, I recognized a couple of guys that I had gone to school with: Joseph Chaiben and Kamil Alasfar. They had both grown beards, and both looked tired and dirty. Joseph's Kalashnikov had the Virgin Mary on its wooden butt; Kamil was holding a sniper machine gun. When Joseph saw me, he aimed at me and said, Trouble students are not allowed here. He smiled and we shook hands.

We sat on sandbags and barrels. Joseph took me to one side and showed me the enemy's position. There, he said. You see that large container? They hide behind it. Listen! He shouted, Hassan, you son of a dog!

A man answered from the other side and exchanged curses.

Did he just curse my sister? Joseph asked Kamil.

You do not have a sister.

Still, he insulted my honour.

Joseph cranked his gun. With a smirk on his face he pointed the rifle in Hassan's direction and shot a few rounds. The whole area went aflame. Bullets flew left and right, back and forth. I dug behind the sandbags; empty, warm bullets flew from Joseph's machine and landed at my feet. When everyone stopped shooting we heard Hassan's voice from the other side. He shouted something about a prostitute, about Christian mothers. Everyone laughed.

George came out of a nearby building with a rifle in his hand. He had a big smile and was laughing with Khalil. Khalil put his arm around George's shoulders and they walked away.

I waited and listened to Joseph telling me about the last two nights, how heavy the fighting had been, how the bombs had fallen like rain and how they had been forced to hold their ground. They could not move, the food truck did not show up, and they were hungry and out of cigarettes; ammunition was getting low and the *Majalis* (militia headquarters) did not care to send more men. He complained, puffed his cigarette, and said, We are not organized. Then he led me inside the building and offered me a cigarette.

Remember our teacher, Souad? he laughed. Her legs, he said. She had nice long legs.

She is in France, I said.

Yeah, I know, he said. Got married to that French teacher. They all want to get married to Frenchmen.

He pulled out his gun and gave it to me. Here, shoot a few rounds, maybe you will get lucky and hit Hassan in the ass. I scared the hell out of him the other day. He was taking a shit on the other side. I was on the second floor, and I saw him, so I rushed and took the sniper gun from Kamil and shot between his legs. He was running with his pants down.

You did not kill him?

No. No. We promised each other that when this war ends we will have a drink.

I refused to take the gun; Joseph shook his head and said, You were always quiet. You are a calm man . . . though I remember you when you had a fight with the Baa'liny brothers at school. You were vicious. Not many boys wanted to mess with you. So what are you doing here?

I came with George to see Khalil.

Are you guys joining?

No. I shook my head.

The forces used to be all volunteers, but now you have to sign up and you are paid. We are turning into more of an army than a militia. Now we even have to wear uniforms. When the war started everyone was in jeans. The top commander, Al-Rayess, has a grand plan. Come back sometime and visit us.

★　★　★

On the drive home to George's place, I asked George what Khalil wanted.

Nothing, he said. Just to talk.

Just to talk?

Khalil knows.

About what?

About our game.

Abou-Nahra knows too?

No. Khalil wants a cut.

How did he find out?

He used to work at the poker place, so he suspected it. He tricked me; first he says that he has a message from Abou-Nahra, and that Abou-Nahra knows. He says there is a counter in the machine. Then he offers to talk on my behalf to Abou-Nahra. If I give the money back to the militia, he says, they will forgive and forget the whole thing. When I said that I do not have the money any more, he switched. He said that he is the only one who knows and that he needs a cut.

Where does Khalil live? I asked George.

Down by the lower bridge.

Where?

Above Appo. The *lahm ba'ajin* place.

He lives alone?

Yeah.

Tell him OK, we will give him a cut.

I walked down to the lower bridge and watched Khalil's house.

I entered the store below his house and ordered

two *lahm ba'ajin*. I ate them, and drank *iran*. Then I walked up the stairs looking for Khalil's name on a buzzer.

When I could not find his name anywhere, I left and went straight back to my house.

At twelve noon the next day, George came to my place. My mother, the Armenian, offered him food. She kissed his cheeks and told him about his mother. Your mother was a wonderful lady, God save her soul, a real lady. She would be so proud to see what a good and handsome man you turned out to be, George.

Then my mother asked George about his aunt Nabila, and his distant uncle and his family. She poured a lot of food onto George's plate, asked him to eat well, and repeated familiar words: You people do not know how to use those spices, like us Armenians.

George called my mother *tante*, kissed her hand, and ate well.

After the meal we went to my room. George stretched out on my bed. I lay on the sofa.

How much does Khalil want?

Half. That leaves you and me with a quarter each.

Half? Does he know I am in on it?

He knows someone else must be in on it.

Tell him to meet you under the bridge, I said.

He won't come. Khalil is a snake.

Okay. Then tell him that we will go to see him down on the front line.

★ ★ ★

Late that night, a man named Samir Al-Afhameh was attacked by a chihuahua on his way home. Samir Al-Afhameh, a respectable man who had once owned a law office in the destroyed downtown Beirut, now unemployed and too proud to work at something else, lived on whatever little money his son sent him from Kentucky.

The pack of dogs growled at him when he passed next to the mountain of garbage. The chihuahua who attacked him had once belonged to Madame Kharazi, who fled to Paris in a hurry, taking a taxi to the checkpoint that divided East and West Beirut. From there, through some rich connection that she had in West Beirut, she was taken to the airport by an ex-army Muslim colonel who knew her husband from before the war. The little dog attacked Mr Samir by order of his three-legged boss.

The next day Mr Samir went to the right-wing militia centre and talked to the men there about the chihuahua attack and the pack of dogs that had invaded his street. He warned them of the dogs' ambition to take over the Christian enclave using the power of their sharp teeth and a well-developed intimidation technique called growling, backed by a garbage mountain to feed them through and through until rabies made their eyes red and saliva dropped through their unbrushed gums.

Mr Samir was dismissed by a local brute commander who walked with open feet like a duck, wore heavy boots in heat or cold weather, whose smell assaulted your nostrils, whose petty theft of vegetables and poultry was reminiscent of a medieval monk on the crusaders' path.

Mr Samir, the advocate schooled by Jesuit priests with long, black robes who recorded every detail meticulously, and who had taught him French and discipline, lifted his eye-glasses and walked straight to Nabila's house. He climbed her stairs and knocked at her door.

Nabila opened the door and made an appearance barefoot and wearing diminutive shorts. This made her thighs look rounder and more luscious than ever. She amended her voice and her hair when she saw Mr Samir's large body, his legal status, his tail that wagged with fury and, at that moment, excitement. Mr Samir dropped his head in reverence and uttered, solemnly, a long monologue worthy of a corrupt judge and a pack of hyenas sitting on jury benches, waiting for leftovers from a lioness with hungry cubs under an African tree.

Excuse me, Madame Nabila. But I must tell everyone what is happening in our neighbourhood. You see, I was attacked by the most beautiful pack of dogs last night. Yes, we might all die any minute from falling bombs and bullets, but if we get rabies from these expensive dogs we might have an epidemic here. I came specifically to you because I know that your nephew has a gun and that he has friends in the militia. Maybe he knows someone in the higher ranks who can do something about it. If I had a gun or knew how to use one, I would get rid of them all. There are kids and women who might be attacked, and there is a pile of garbage not too far from your house, and those dogs might attack even you or anyone . . .

Oh my God, absolutely, Mr Samir, we have to do something about it. I am terrified of dogs.

Yes.

Please come in.

Well . . . eh . . . okay.

Were do they come from? We never had dogs loose like that before.

Well, there is no government, no law, no order any more, and everyone throws garbage on the streets, some even throw it from the balcony. The other day . . . the people above us . . .

God help us . . . what a life we have now.

Things have changed, Madame Nabila. Everything has changed . . . There is no respect in this war . . .

Coffee, Professor Samir?

Well, no, thank you.

Oh yes . . . We have to have coffee. It will calm your nerves.

Okay, no sugar, please . . . We must get rid of them, Madame Nabila, absolutely.

I will tell Gargourty about it. How is your son?

He is well, thank you.

He is in America?

Yes, in Kentucky. The telephone is hard.

You know, the lines . . . He tries to call. He is always worried . . . They see the news there . . . And we cannot call him, my wife tries for hours . . .

America, all our trouble comes from America, Mr Samir.

Well, yes, that dog Kissinger's plan, Madame Nabila.

The oil, they want the oil in the region, Mr Samir.

Yes, Madame Nabila. Yes, you are right. Your coffee is very good.

Sahtayn. How is your wife?

Well, she sits all day complaining, Madame Nabila. You know, since Ziad left she cries all the time.

Your wife is a wonderful lady, Mr Samir. The other day I saw her on the street. I did not stop and talk to her . . . You know, Mr Samir, we do not know when the bombing will start any more. We are always rushing . . . I listen to the news all day . . .

I am sorry, but I have to leave, Madame Nabila.

Yes, may God be with you.

The dogs have to go.

I will talk to Gargourty.

Au revoir.

Nabila picked up the phone and called Abou-Nahra.

Dogs!? Abou-Nahra said. Is it the time for talk of dogs now? Is that what you called me for?

Do you know what rabies is, About? It makes you bark like a dog. They will put a piece of wood in your mouth for you to bite. Yeah, you will be driving your big Range Rover with a piece of wood in your mouth . . . Oh well, maybe it is not a good idea after all, Abou . . . Do something about it . . . Do something for the people besides shooting them and taking their money.

And Nabila hung up the phone, lit a cigarette, and noticed she was alone in an empty house, all alone in a war, and surrounded by dogs, human dogs, dogs in men's masks, dogs with guns, dogs in banker suits, dogs that pee on one's couch and pant their filthy breath on one's breast. They are all dogs, men; especially men. Nothing but unfaithful dogs.

Late the next night we heard close-range shots in our neighbourhood. The men went down in their pyjamas, with guns and long knives in their hands.

They are killing dogs! The words of the Christians flew from one balcony to another. Two jeeps carrying seven militiamen surrounded the dogs. Dog massacre! Dog slaughter! An Afghani hound bitch was executed for treason, while in Paris her beloved owner was on all fours on a silk bedsheet, backing up her secret lover, Pierre, a French painter, in his artistic endeavours. A cocker spaniel was pursued by a fat fighter, while his mommy was buying filet mignon in the Champs Élysées for an evening of wine and debauchery. A German shepherd was slaughtered like a sheep in a wolf story, while his adoptive parents were drinking beer at a long table in a European bar filled with men singing Bavarian songs. The chihuahua was missed twice because of his small size, but was finally shot at close range, under a car, while his mother, in Venice, discussed the origin of silk in a chic salon over espresso. The three-legged leader died alone, an orphan, on top of a mountain of rubbish, propped up by a piece of metal, a few empty hummus cans, and a box of Belgian detergent.

During the massacre, Samir the lawyer stood beside the jeep, pointing his finger, reading aloud the execution orders and shutting the dogs' eyes. He tied their paws with long leather leashes to crucifixes carried by Roman soldiers with skirts and open sandals; he stuck last cigarettes between their loose canines; he swung his sword up and down with every shot, delirious, salivating dog food, and shouting, The small one, get the small one! It is under the car . . . He is dangerous . . . Give me the gun, I will do it . . .

Do not leave any . . . They should all go! he shouted in his pyjamas that night, a night known ever since as 'The night of the big moon and the final howl.'

Dog blood filled our streets in rivers of drifting bones and urine.

The Christians won the battle, the battle of the hundred dogs.

★   ★   ★

George came the next day to pick me up. We drove down to the green line to meet Khalil. We both brought money. On the way there, in the middle of a deserted street, we stopped under a bridge, away from the snipers' sharp eyes.

We put the money in a bag.

I will show him the money, George said to me.

At the checkpoint, we were stopped by a few men surrounded by sandbags. A young man with a rifle asked me where I was going. I told him we were going to see Khalil the rooster. He made us wait while he phoned Abou-Haddid. We were cleared.

When you pass that main street with the burned van in the middle, drive as fast as you can. The sniper can see you from the tower there, the boy said to us.

Before we got to Danger Street, George stopped. Hold on tight, he said.

He lifted the bike on one wheel and we zoomed straight to the compound.

Joseph met us. I shook hands with him while George went looking for Khalil. He found him, and they both disappeared into a vacant building.

I talked to Joseph. He had a toothache, he said, pressing his hand against his left cheek. I have been sipping *araq* to calm the pain.

I told him about a dentist who would give him a good price. He said he knew one as well. But it is the electricity, he said. No electricity . . . The last time I went to the dentist the electricity was suddenly cut off and I sat in the chair waiting, in pain.

How is Hassan on the other side? I asked.

Let us see. Hassan, Joseph shouted.

Hassan answered with a series of affectionate, dirty curses.

He just insulted your sister again, I said playfully.

Yeah, here, shoot him and save my honour, brother. Joseph giggled. He handed me his rifle.

I held it with my right hand and cranked it with my left hand. I aimed it in the air and shot toward Hassan's side, while Joseph cursed the vagina that gave Hassan birth.

Hassan fired back at us from the other side. We dug in, and then I stuck the rifle in an opening in the sandbags and shot some more. Joseph stood up and called to Hassan, promising to turn him into ham. The whole front line went ablaze, and everyone started to shoot. Abou-Haddid came running with a ten millimetre in both hands. He sang profanities as he shot a long round from the bullet belt that covered his strong shoulders. Joseph was smiling the entire time. He grabbed the rifle from my hand, changed the magazines for me, and shouted in my ear, I see you're enjoying this!

At that moment, screams came from the building, screams for help. It was George's voice. As we ran toward him, I could hear him screaming, He is hit, he is hit. Khalil was flung over George's shoulders, bleeding, dripping blood along the tips of his fingers. Abou-Haddid ran to George, lifted Khalil's body, and laid it in the back of the jeep. George climbed in beside Khalil. I took the motorcycle, and Joseph hopped on behind me, and we drove like madmen, honking all the way to the hospital. I could see Khalil's wounded body bouncing inside the jeep. George cushioned his head and hung on to him, looking away. I sped in front of the jeep while, from behind me, Joseph shot in the air, clearing the way.

When we arrived at the emergency ward, Abou-Haddid lifted up Khalil and rushed inside. He laid Khalil's loose body on a rolling bed and screamed for a doctor. When no one showed up, he pulled out his gun and shot in the hallway; white paint and chips of dust fell from the ceiling onto his red face. Two nurses ran over and rushed Khalil through the hallways of the hospital.

Khalil died.

On the highway home, George drove the motor-cycle slowly. Behind George, I opened the bag with the money, split the cash, and hid it from the wind. I slipped George's share into the inside pocket of his jacket, next to his gun.

George, I said the next day while we were sitting in a café, smoking and drinking coffee, Khalil's funeral is on Wednesday. Are you going?

No, he said, and looked at me with piercing

eyes. I do not kill the bird and dance with its feathers.

On wednesday I went down to the street under the bridge. On the way I saw Khalil's photo pasted on a shoemaker's door and on concrete walls. *The hero Khalil Al-Deeq, martyred on the front line defending his beloved country*, the poster said. I walked on and went up to the roof of a building opposite Khalil's home. I perched like a hawk, watching men entering the building, hearing women in black wailing sacred chants in a room filled with fainting mothers, red-eyed, weeping sisters, pious grandmothers. Militiamen filled the streets.

I saw Abou-Nahra get out of his jeep and walk straight to the coffin. He shook hands with his sunglasses on. I wanted to see his eyes.

Funerals are all the same, I thought. Men and women were segregated. The house of the deceased accepted the women and the neighbour's house was open to men. And I was on the roof, a vulture that watched from above and landed only to eat.

When the coffin came down the narrow stairs, held by mighty young men who fought over its gold-metal handles and lifted it on their shoulders to walk it back to earth, the women's wails intensified. Balconies throughout the neighbourhood were filled with people; the roofs were covered with curious and silent faces. Khalil's battalion stood in line, aimed their rifles toward a passing cloud, and shot in the air to the slow, migrating coffin.

Men walked behind the coffin, women waved to it. From above, I watched the Christians passing on the road to hell.

CHAPTER 6

The heat made my throat dry; I was lying in my underwear thinking of Rana.

I put on my jeans and I went down the street toward her house. As my foot touched the melting earth, church bells rang. Miracle! Miracle! shouted Wafa and rushed toward the sounds. Issam scratched his head; Boutros looked at the sky. I walked toward the church and saw a crowd gathered around its door, old ladies in black beating their saggy chests. I grabbed Salah, the plumber, by the hand, and in a low voice I asked what was happenig. He answered, There is a young girl who saw the Virgin Mary hovering in the sky. She opened her robe and shielded us all from the Muslims' falling bombs. The girl's hands are secreting holy oil.

The church was packed. Mumbles fused with prayers, prayers combusted with the holy waters and burned in candles. Collective chants slid toward the skies.

Like a reptile with moist skin, I slipped into the mob. I made my way toward the front of the church, separating the crippled from their mothers, the blind from their canes, the faces in tears from their sweeping palms. Above the kneeling heads I moved forward, toward the golden icons, then stood to the side and watched: she was there, standing like a statue, a young girl I had never seen before. She was looking up to the ceiling; her hands were open and shiny. She was young, in her teens, and her eyes shone with madness and evasion. A small smirk was on her lips, and she looked hazy and eerie.

The priest puffed incense around the girl. People crossed themselves, and an old lady rushed forward and touched the girl's hand. The priest pulled the old lady back and drove her away, but then the crowd moved forward and reached for the girl. A few men moved in and pushed the crowd back, forming a shield to protect the young woman. The girl was taken back behind the altar. The low hums and hysterical cries, the reaching hands and beating of chests, the fog of incense, the superstitious shrieks, the sight of pious bodies on crushed knees, the unbearable heat, all these made me seek the open doors. On my way out I grabbed the woman who had touched the girl's hands, held her fingers to my nose to smell, but the old woman liberated her hand, pushed me back, and shouted at me: Faith! Faith! I made my way out of the crowd like the spear of a warrior in retreat.

For days, people flocked to the church from all over the city. The tolling of the bell muffled the bangs of bombs. My mother's radio and the ring of bells deafened me.

In the evening, the sun departed. A bright, round moon arrived and occupied its place. It hovered above the Virgin Mary, made her blue dress glow white, and formed a halo above her head. Down below, a crowd rushed toward the church, bounced, splashed, and retreated from its walls like the tide.

Rana and I were naked in George's room at his apartment. Rana's hands were dry and warm, her thighs wet as silk sheets dipped in holy oil. She covered herself and listened as I dreamed about the pigeons in Roma.

You want to go to Roma?

I am thinking about it.

And what, you'll leave me here?

No, you can come with me.

And what would I do in Roma?

Study, walk the streets, and come back to me.

And how would we do this?

I am working on it, I said.

Rana got up and went to the kitchen. There were dirty dishes in the sink. She squeezed soap onto a sponge, poured water into the sink from a bucket, and rinsed the dishes.

I cannot stand dirty dishes, she said. It drives me crazy. Go outside and see if there are any nosy neighbours on the stairs; I have to go home.

I opened the door and looked outside. There is no one, I told her.

Rana covered herself and ran down the stairs.

Close the door, she whispered fiercely on her way down. Go inside! Close the door, someone will see me.

I kept the door open, smiling and looking at her.

Later that evening George joined me at his place.

From the balcony I saw him drive up in a jeep. He was wearing a militia uniform and holding an M-16. When he got out of the jeep he switched his rifle from one hand to the other. He knocked at his own door. Is Rana still there? he asked me.

She left. New clothes? I asked.

He did not answer. He laid his rifle on the sofa, took off his boots, and said, Abou-Nahra called me in.

And?

He asked me what was happening down at the casino. I think he smells something.

I doubt it.

Well, he asked me to join. He looked me straight in the eyes and said it's better for everyone. You know what he meant, don't you?

So you got alarmed and joined? Maybe he meant that you might lose your job.

No, I know what he meant. I was there.

Where does Abou-Nahra live? I asked George.

He is always surrounded by bodyguards, Bassam. Forget about it. Listen, we better cool it with the poker machines for now. He held his rifle closer to his chest, against his khaki shirt, under his chin. Then he pointed it at me and smiled.

Hold it. See? It's light as a feather. He took off his clothes, went to the bathroom. Fucking water, I heard him cursing.

He pulled on his shirt and pants, went up to the roof, and came back with a bucket. While I poured water on his head, he washed under his armpits. When he was finished washing, he dabbed cologne under his chin.

I am going to meet the Broumana woman, he told me.

She called?

He nodded and combed his straight black hair. Are you coming?

No, I am staying. But leave me the handgun.

He tossed it on the sofa and asked no questions.

I tucked the gun under my belt and walked over to Joseph Chaiben's house. I climbed up the open stairs, smearing the dirty marble with my foot-prints. Joseph lived in one of those old Lebanese houses, a mixture of Florentine and Arabic archi-tecture, that are overwhelmed by larger, modern buildings with mechanical elevators and large balconies.

I knocked at Joseph's door. His mother opened. I greeted her and asked after her health. She invited me in and called to her son. Joseph had been asleep. He entered in his shorts, a sleeveless white cotton shirt, and plastic slippers that complemented his mother's cheap tablecloth. As he greeted me, his mother brought me a drink, apologizing for not having ice, complaining about the water shortage, the war . . . life . . . Her words echoed my mother's.

When Joseph and I went up to the roof, Joseph's mother shouted from below, The roofs are dangerous; there are snipers everywhere! Come down here; talk in the room. I will leave; come back down.

But the roof had no walls and we wanted no echoes, so we ignored her. I showed Joseph the gun and asked him if he knew of someone selling a gun like it. He held it, took off the magazine, put it back on, cranked the gun, aimed it toward West Beirut and fired.

Beretta, I said. Nine millimetre, ten shots. Clean, never used in combat.

I will look into it.

How are Khalil's parents doing? I said.

His sister saw me on the street the other day. I was coming back from the front line in my uniform, gear and all, and when she saw me she started to shout, You people killed my brother. You are all thugs and criminals to take young men to war. He was seventeen, she said. A baby, seventeen!

Joseph shook his head and inspected the gun again.

Do you still go down to the front line? I asked.

Yeah, he said. Abou-Nahra won't let me leave. You know, once you're in, you're in.

And what does Abou-Nahra think about Khalil's death?

He asked a lot of questions but never said anything to me.

I promised Joseph some oily, shiny hash; he smiled and said he would do his best to find a good gun for me.

When we went down, his mother was gone; Joseph went back inside the house.

That day, as I remember, there was a ceasefire and few clouds.

The next day I borrowed George's motorcycle. I met Rana on the outskirts of the neighbourhood, at the corner of a building filled with people who had never seen our faces before. She mounted the motorcycle behind me and we drove straight to the mountains. She clasped both her arms around my waist. I drove on gravel roads and into the belly of the hills. When we stopped, I handed her the gun, wrapped my arms around her shoulders, put my hands over hers, and we both extended our arms and took aim at rusty cans. She fired, and laughed. Then she liberated herself from my arms, pushed me back and took the gun by herself, aimed and shot. She smiled and walked toward me, swinging her hips, waving the gun in the air. She pointed it at my chest. Flipping her long lashes playfully, she said: Now that I have a gun, I will follow you to Roma and shoot you down if you leave without me.

From afar Beirut looked like a stretch of little cement hills, crowded buildings with no roads, no lampposts, no humans.

There, that is the Muslim side, she pointed. I have never met a Muslim. No, wait, there were a couple of Muslim girls in school, but they fled when the war started. Faten, one of their names was, Faten; the other, I can't remember . . . Can't remember.

I held Rana and kissed her neck. The soft, cool breeze made her nipples erect under her thin white cotton shirt. I slipped my hand onto her chest, molested her breasts, and sucked her round, red nipples.

She was anxious, looking around, watching for stray visitors, nature lovers and bird hunters, and when I pushed my hand inside her tight jeans, she said: Bassam, stop. Not here. Bassam, stop!

I did not stop. I was breathing like a hound and I forced myself on her; Rana froze, then gripped my hand and pushed me away. She pointed the gun at me.

When I say stop, you stop! You stop, she shouted in anger.

I walked toward her. I grabbed her wrist, pointed the gun again at my chest, and said, Pull it!

You are hurting my wrist, she said.

I took the gun back, and we both kept our silence, breathing heavily.

Then we drove farther up into the hills. We stopped and looked at the city again. A long, mushroom-shaped cloud sprang from the earth in West Beirut.

A bomb, Rana said to me. Look, a bomb just landed.

More like an explosion, I said.

As we drove back down the hill, Rana's hands caressed my chest. She drove her nail into my flesh and said, I could have shot you here.

My Mother came shuffling up the stairs with bags in her hand: vegetables, meat, bread.

She called me into the kitchen. What is going on between you and Rana? This morning over coffee her mother asked me about you two.

What did she ask?

About your job, and if you are interested in visiting their house with me. She said Rana is at the age to be engaged.

We are just friends, I said.

Don't lie to me, Bassam. Rana is like a daughter to me, and she is not that kind of girl. If you are not serious, do not ruin her future. People talk here. People talk.

I walked away. She shouted at my back, Yeah, just like your father. He always left, and he kept on leaving. A good-for-nothing, he was a good-for-nothing.

I heard the kitchen door slam behind me.

More than ten thousand bombs had landed, and I was stranded between two walls facing my trembling mother. She had refused to go down to the shelter unless I came with her. And I refused to hide underground. I, descended from a long line of mighty warriors, would die only in the open air above an earth of muddy soils and whistling winds!

My mother jumped at every explosion. She called upon one female saint after another but none of them, busy virgins, ever answered her back.

Petra, the little neighbour girl, crawled up the dirty marble stairs and knocked on our door; she looked suspiciously at my glittering sword and warrior face, then covered her lips and whispered a secret in my mother's ear. My mother stood up and walked straight to the bathroom. She came back with a box of Kotex and said, It is empty, *habibti*, but do not worry; come with me.

The little menstruating body stood up, her face a deep, bashful red. She dashed inside, to my mother's bedroom.

I walked down the stairs, out of the building, and across the deserted street toward Abou-Dolly, the grocer. The store was closed, but Abou-Dolly lived with his family in the back. I knocked. The grocer opened the door a crack. He saw me and frowned and asked me what I needed. Kotex, I said. We are closed now, he answered in a dry tone.

It is urgent! I said.

Come in.

I entered the house. It smelled of villagers' soap,

ground coffee, and rotting vegetables that had fallen under the loud fridge, and two cats that fed on brown mice, and the grocer's daughter, Dolly, who was breastfeeding her newborn from her round white breast that made me thirsty. When I stepped in, Dolly covered her baby and her breast in a pink wool quilt. Um-Dolly, the grocer's wife, was there knitting in the corner; his son-in-law, Elias, was wearing suspenders and gazing at the wall and smoking. They were all gathered around two pitiful candles that flickered in a wild, diabolic motion, projecting everyone's shadow on Hades and its burning walls.

Abou-Dolly, a middle-aged man who had never had a son, and whose nickname referred to his older daughter, handed me two packs of Kotex. Which kind do you want? he asked me.

I held both cases close to the candle and smelled them, which made his wife shiver and puff and murmur in objection. What are you smelling them for? Abou-Dolly rushed at me and snatched the boxes. Get out, get out. He started to push me; I shoved him back. His son-in-law picked up a long broomstick and threatened me with it. I snatched back one of the boxes from Abou-Dolly's hand, slipped my other hand behind my waist, and pulled out my gun. I let it hang off my fingers, pointing toward the floor. Um-Dolly shouted, He has a gun! He has a gun! Dolly cut off the jet of warm milk to her baby's lips, which made the baby cry, and rushed into another room.

Clutching the box, I stepped outside the door into the fresh air and walked away. In the background I heard Abou-Dolly shouting, I knew your father, I knew your father, he was a friend of mine, and he would be ashamed to see what his son turned out to be. A thug! Shame on you, insulting me in my own house, in front of my family. A thug! That is what you are, my son, a thug. And he spat on the floor and cursed my generation and my kind.

The thug walked between the buildings, avoiding the falling bombs. The thug crossed streams of sewage that dripped from broken pipes. He walked with a gun in one hand and a box of tender cotton in the other.

The next day, George came by to pick up his motorcycle.

It was parked, tilted toward the earth, over a round pool of dried oil, in the shade in front of the vegetable store, facing the hospital, its back to the church.

I gave George the keys; he dangled the ring from his longest finger and said, Let's go talk.

He drove, and I held on to his waist. We drove down to Quarantina, to the old train tracks where the Kurdish shanty-town had been conquered and demolished by the Christians. Now the earth was flat here, the tin roofs, the little alleys, the pools of sewage all evaporated, vanquished and levelled to the ground. The fighters had been massacred in cold blood. Their women had fled in little boats bouncing on Mediterranean waves, barefoot kids with dripping noses in their arms. It was here that Abou-Nahra and his men had stormed the camp, killed the men and pulled out their golden teeth; it was here that he had gained his reputation as a ruthless commander. His victorious men had pierced the heads of the defeated on bayonets and paraded the streets. Cadavers had been tied to the backs of jeeps, bounced on asphalt roads and hurtled down the little alleys.

The camp was a meadow now, with wild weeds growing from the cadaver compost, ashes of burned walls, and troops of flies that once grazed on blood and empty bullet shells.

Speak, I said. Speak, before the buried under our feet come to life.

I am leaving the poker place, George said. I asked Najib, my distant cousin, to take my place. You can still do the deal. I will show him the trick.

Why are you leaving?

Abou-Nahra asked me to do some work.

What kind of work?

I will be leaving for Israel soon for some training. The forces are establishing relations with the Jews down south.

It is a mistake, I whispered.

No, Bassam, we are alone in this war, and our people are being massacred every day. And you . . . whose grandfather was butchered . . . your father killed . . . you . . . you . . . We will unite with the devil to save our land. How are we to make the Syrians and the Palestinians leave?

I am fleeing and leaving this land to its devils, I said.

You believe in nothing.

Thieves and thugs like us, I said, since when have we ever believed in anything?

We drove down the highway to the seashore. The roads were empty; it was a summer day, and the wind was warm. We sat at the shore and watched the water.

Little boats rocked, modest waves advanced, and still we sat. Night fell, and we lit fires on thin paper, and smoked and gazed and watched and hallucinated, and laughed and smoked some more. We burned the joints down to the tips of our fingers, sealed the embers with our nails. I had a vision of trees and plains, and a house – an open house, and shadows and a sun that travelled in a straight line and not in a circle, and a moon that stayed still and was lit at night by candles, by stars, by nothing but tiny holes through which light passed and landed on an ocean. The earth smelled of wetness, but the grass was brown, dying and changing and floating on salty water. I got up and walked, and I met a fisherman; we passed each other in utter silence – not a glance, not a glimpse. I had a dream of a table, a woman with dyed hands, and a broken chair, all under one roof. I saw doors that I had to open. I walked toward the first door and pulled it with all my strength; I entered and rushed toward the second door, but it was locked. I stayed there for days, begging the door to open. Then I fell asleep and dreamt of the door opening. A naked woman with a bag smiled at me and said, Take off your garments. I looked down and saw my robe turning to water. I gathered the water and gave it to her. She held it in her hands and poured it in my eyes. Now, she said, go through the third door and if you see your father tell him that you left your garment. I saw two paths. I will take the narrow path, I said. I had another dream, and in that dream I was in a river, I held a piece of bread that I threw to a bird. I crossed the river and found the fourth door. I pushed it with all my might, but it wouldn't open. I touched it gently with my finger, and it opened. I entered into a garden with a chair and a book. I sat on the chair and smoked. Then I sang, and another door opened to me. I rushed through it and passed through emptiness and no trees, no tables, no chairs, no bird wing, no moon nor lights, no thoughts. I stood still and closed my eyes. I dreamt of a large flower. I smelled it. I climbed its stem and made a bed out of its petals. Then I slept and had another dream, a vision of a friend immersed in a pool of light and blood.

George and I drove back, the road ahead of us brightened by the single light that shone under our numb chests, our knuckles, and our heavy, red eyes. We drove toward the darkened city lit by dim lanterns hung on barricades. The city's feeble rays bounced off shiny soldiers' boots.

When I arrived home, the phone rang, but I did not pick it up. I lay down on my bed. I could not sleep. I pulled out the gun from beneath my shirt and hid it under the mattress. Noises came from below: cat fights, occasional rushing feet, murmurs, quiet murmurs that entered my mind and my dreams and turned into familiar words.

Suddenly my mother's hands were rocking me, pulling my cover and begging me to wake up.

Come down; they are targeting the neighbourhood. Come down and away from the window. How can you fall asleep like that? The bombs are all around us.

Nahla, our neighbour, was with her, and she pleaded with me as well. Have pity on your mother. Come down with us to the shelter. She has waited for you all day and all night. How can you be so thoughtless? She did not sleep all night. Where were you?

I will stay between these two walls, I said. You two go down; I'll be fine here.

No, come down! We need a man in the shelter. Come down now, my love. On your grandfather's grave, come down!

We heard a loud blast. A bomb fell nearby. The women shrieked and threw themselves on the floor. Close! This is a close one, they said and got up and ran into the hallway. Glass and chunks of stone fell from above, onto the street. My mother was shaking. I looked in her eyes and noticed that wrinkles had surfaced to channel her tears down her sunken cheeks.

The kids, my kids! Nahla cried.

I grabbed Nahla's hand to stop her from running outside. The second one must be coming, I said. Don't move!

Nahla tried to run, but I held her. She fought in my arms like a captive beast. Then she scratched my face and escaped. I followed her down the stairs. In hysterics, she shouted her kids' names all the way down to the street filled with broken glass. A sudden loud, penetrating boom shook the building. I felt it pressing on my chest. I heard the noise of delayed glass falling; I saw a fog of smoke that tasted of old dust and cruel soil. The smell of powder and burned bread pushed me through the smoke and up the stairs where, breathless, I cried: *Mother*.

PART II

BEIRUT

CHAPTER 7

My parents, who hated each other in life, now rested together in wooden boxes under the same earth.

They had fought and screamed at each other when my father came back late at night with alcohol on his breath and a pair of defeated gambler's hands that slapped my mother's face, and blackened her eyes, and chased her to the kitchen under flying saucers and above broken plates. Now still, two corpses devoured by slimy carnivorous worms, they were at each other's throats under the moist earth.

I threw the first grain of dust over my mother's coffin, then turned and walked back toward the house, away from the repetitive chants, and white smoke of incense, and tears.

For days, neighbours and friends came and knocked at my door, but I didn't open it.

I smoked. Somehow, the quiet of clinking pots, the silence of the radio, the absence of the subtle rustle of a broom, the solitude, gave me tranquility.

The wind blew as it pleased through the two

large holes in the house. Only the wind entered; only the wind could. Late one night when I opened the door on my way out to buy cigarettes, I found a plate of bread on the doorstep. The neighbours had left it there, after their knuckles had turned red and tired from knocking at my door.

I walked the streets and found my way down to the cemetery. I smoked, then climbed over the fence and stood in front of a pile of soil. It was still not shovelled down. I stood and listened to my parents' murmurs. Or was it the winds stroking the white stone crosses?

Later that night, Nabila and George broke the lock on my door and entered the apartment. Nabila wore black. She rushed toward me.

Skinny, she said. Look at you, how yellow and skinny you are. You have to eat. I brought you food. She sat at the edge of my bed and said, You have to eat. Please, Bassam, eat.

George stood quietly, a little farther away. He strolled between the pieces of broken furniture, looked through the open walls. Then he pulled out a box of cigarettes and offered me one. When he struck the match, Nabila hissed at him, Enough cigarettes. He has to eat. Look how yellow he is.

The next day, I went back to work at the port. Abou-Tariq, the foreman, walked slowly toward me. He gave me his condolences, and I thanked him. I could see he was waiting for signs of sadness or for me to shed tears like the salty waves that dropped below our feet and fractured on the concrete edges of the dock. But I had no sadness to spare or parade. If anything, the death of my mother had liberated me. Now I would leave nothing behind. Her death had made me closer to birds and farther away from humans. Birds fly, and I aspired to my own flight. I wanted to stray, with my head close to the ground, watching the passing pebbles, and smelling dust. Now I was a creature closer to dogs than to men.

At the end of the day, I entered my apartment building and saw Rana sitting on the stairs. I walked past her without saying a word. She followed me up the stairs and into my bedroom. Then she walked around the house and began to pick up pieces of broken furniture and scattered stones.

Leave it, I said.

No! she shouted and started to cry. Then she held my hand and said, You have to fix the house. You hear? You hear me?

She picked up objects, and shed tears, and shouted at me, Days pass and you hardly say a word.

I kept silent.

Enough! Say something! Say something! She pushed me with open palms.

I tried to leave; she blocked my way. No! You are not leaving before you say something to me. No.

I pushed her away; she bounced back and obstructed my way again: No, no. No more silence.

I pushed her again. She slapped me. I held her hand and forced her hard onto the dusty floor, and then I walked down the stairs and into the city.

When I met Najib at the casino, it was morning and the gambling machines were still unplugged. The place smelled of the last night's smoke, unwashed whisky glasses, and the gamblers' heavy breath.

I am George's friend, I said.

He nodded as he came from behind the bar and plugged in one of the machines.

Later that afternoon, Najib and I met on the church stairs.

He was more nervous now than he had been in the morning.

I walked past him and asked him to follow me. He hesitated, waited a minute, then followed me down the stairs.

The church corner smelled of piss and the dew of old city walls. I handed him the money. He counted it, slipped it in his pocket, and abruptly asked me, When are you coming again?

Friday morning, as usual. Did George tell you to bring me whisky if you suspect anything?

Yeah, yeah, he told me everything, Najib said. He turned away, bouncing up the stairs in a hurry.

Friday, I called out after him.

* * *

Ten thousand coffins had slipped underground and the living still danced above ground with firearms in their hands. Over the next few days I bought a gun from Joseph, and fixed the house walls. Winter was coming and the migrating winds were no longer welcome. Rain fell and soaked the earth and bathed my parents in soft mud. I smoked all day as I lay in my bed. The house was quiet, and I was alone.

One afternoon I picked up my mother's radio and held it in my arms.

I pulled back the cover. Inside, the wires were green and yellow. The speaker was round and mute, tinny silver metal glued on green plastic sheets. I looked for Fairuz, but she was singing in Paris.

On Friday when I went to the casino, Najib was dismissive. He made me wait for my change; finally he injected a small amount in the machine, less than the usual. While I was playing, another young man entered. Through the reflection in the glass of my machine, I saw Najib waving his hand to the man. The man made a sign to Najib and left.

I cashed my money and left.

I crossed the street and waited in the doorway of a nearby building.

I saw the young man going back into the casino. I took a long look at him and I waited. I smoked and I waited. When the man came out of the casino I followed him from afar until he got into his car and drove away.

The next time I saw Najib, he had new leather shoes, a leather jacket, and gel in his hair.

We met downstairs under the church. I gave him his half of the money I had made.

Najib counted it, then calmly said to me, There is more.

What did you say? I said.

There is more. You heard me.

No, that is it, I said. There is no more. I stood closer to him and looked him in the eyes.

He looked back at me and said, Yes, there is.

Inject more on the screen and there will be more for you, I said.

He said nothing but turned and left. When he got to the top of the stairs, he looked down at me and said, Najib always gets what is his.

I said, Let the little kid Najib do whatever he has to do.

He will. Najib spat on the floor and walked away with his peacock walk.

A couple of days later, I went to King Falafel for a sandwich and a Pepsi. I saw George and Abou-Nahra eating. I should have known they were there by the strip of power cars stretched on the sidewalk, but I was hungry and not thinking. I tried to dodge them, but it was too late; George saw me and called me over. I walked straight to him and we kissed. Abou-Nahra had on his Ray-Ban sunglasses, so you couldn't tell whether he was looking at you. George introduced me; the commander smiled, asked me to sit, and invited me for a sandwich. I declined, but he insisted, shouting to the boy behind the counter. So I ate.

Abou-Nahra was surrounded by men I recognized: Kamil, Joseph, and Abou-Haddid, Khalil's friend, who waved from a table behind us and asked me if I still worked at the port.

It is slow these days, I said.

George told Abou-Nahra that my father had been the founder of a radio station in the 1950s. Abou-Nahra said he had known my late father and my uncle Naeem. The communist, he said and smiled. He left us for the other side. How is he doing?

We never hear from him, I said.

We were on the same volleyball team. Did you know that?

No. I must have been a kid at the time.

You are still a kid now. He laughed.

When Abou-Nahra was ready to leave, his men stood up. Some crushed the paper wraps in their hands and shoved their sandwiches into their mouths. Abou-Nahra put his arm around my neck. He tapped one finger in his palm slowly and said in his deep voice, George, bring this fighter to the centre one day to join. We don't want him to join the other side like his uncle. We always need good young men.

George was evasive; he muttered something in a low voice. I watched Abou-Nahra. I still wanted to see his eyes. George winked at me, went out with the men, and then came back inside and sat across from me. When I finished eating, we walked down the street to a jeep parked on the sidewalk.

That's Khalil's jeep, I said.

Yeah, he won't need it any more.

We drove down to the stretch of road under the bridge. We parked. George kept his M-16 by his side. I moved back in my seat, just enough to feel my own gun pressing against my back. We could hear the sound of rushing cars from above.

When are you leaving? George asked, looking straight at me.

Not yet.

Najib visited me last night. He said that you owe him money.

Your cousin is a liar, I said. He has another person in the deal.

I'll talk to him. How is Rana?

She's fine.

Listen, I'm leaving next week for Israel. We are going by ship. I will leave you the keys to the apartment. If Nabila asks, tell her that I went camping in the mountains with some friends.

George slipped his hand onto his rifle. He pulled it out slowly and placed it on the back seat. Then he turned on the jeep's engine and we drove back to the neighbourhood.

When I stepped out of his jeep, George looked at me and said, I will talk to my cousin.

I waited for Najib at the top of the hill outside the city, as we had arranged earlier that day.

He came in a car with two other guys. From far away I could hear their loud music. Dust flew up and smothered the scent of the idiot's perfumed aftershave and hair gel. He got out of the car. I watched from behind a tree as he walked uphill in his flat Italian shoes, slipping on the rocks, carrying his shiny leather jacket on his arm. I let him pass me by; when I saw his back, I walked slowly toward him. I grabbed his jacket and threw it on the ground, and I pushed him against a tree.

Najib jerked in fear. I looked at his hands; they were empty. I ran my hand along his waist; he was clean.

Who is in the car? I asked.

My friends, he said, startled. He smelled of alcohol.

Why did you bring your friends?

We are on our way to Broumana.

No one should have come with you.

They do not know about our deal.

I slipped his share of money into his pocket and said to him, You are reckless and acting like an idiot. One day Abou-Nahra will find out and he will put a bullet in your head. Not your cousin or your mother will stop him from doing it. Now, go and say that you went for a piss. That's what you told them, right?

He did not answer.

I walked up the hill and looked down into the valley. Then I looked at the sea in front of me, the sea I'd have to plunge into and slip beneath and swim through one day, to reach other shores and leave this place.

CHAPTER 8

George came back from Israel.

He called me, and I went to see him at his place. Abou-Haddid opened the door. He kissed me, held my neck, and made me sit next to him, tapping his hand on my shoulder. George had a deep desert tan. They were both sniffing cocaine from a flat glass surface.

Do you want a line of dried milk? George pointed at the coffee table.

No, I will pass.

George wore a T-shirt with three Hebrew letters on it. He looked muscular, quieter, and his hair was shaved. He moved slower and seemed more intense. He poured whisky and talked of the camp in the desert and the training.

When you sneak up on an enemy from behind to slash his throat, you should hold him by the chin and not his mouth, because he will bite your hand, right? So we had to practise it. Paul Jeouriege – you know, the one who lives in Karm Al-Zeitoun? You know him, Bassam, he drives the white Fiat with the high spoiler – anyway, he put his hand on Beebo's mouth, not his chin, right? So what does Beebo do? He bit his hand and he wouldn't let go, and Paul was screaming in pain, *Won yallah shid ya, Beeho, shid mitl ma shad bayak awwal laylah* (Push, push, Beebo, in the same way your father pushed on his first night).

George and Abou-Haddid both laughed.

Listen to George's story, Abou-Haddid said to me. Listen. On your sister's honour, listen. This guy is a big *fannas* (liar).

George was high and smiling. He looked at me and said, By your father's lost soul, Bassam, tell Abou-Haddid about Nicole, that young woman who gave me her number in Broumana. You were with me then. Tell this guy.

Yeah, I was there. She is *hamshah, shalkhah*, I said.

Shalkhah, right? said George. Well, I gave her a call. An older man answered the phone, right? I thought it was her father, but when I asked her, Nicole said no, he is her husband.

Should I call you later? I asked her.

No, she said, not to worry, and she kept on talking, natural, like no one is there, right?

So I kept on calling her every day, and sometimes I asked her what she was wearing, and she would tell me she had nothing on, or some lace underwear, or sometimes just a T-shirt.

So we started to talk dirty, while her husband is still at home, right? When I asked if her husband was there once, she said that he was listening on the other line. So I am thinking, What the fuck? You know, maybe he is not a real man, right?

The next time I called he recognized my voice and said, How are you, George? Come and visit us sometime. Then Nicole took the phone and we started to talk, natural.

George approached the tray, kneeled, and took a snort of cocaine. He inhaled through one nostril while blocking the other with his index finger. Then he continued:

So I went to their home in Surssock. You know, one of those fancy houses. A maid opened the door. The man, who maybe is in his sixties, maybe older, he looked like her father. He had white hair and was dressed in his *robe de chambre* and slippers, and he was smoking a big cigar. He invited me in and started to talk to me in French, right? *Bonjour, George, comment ça va?* He showed me around the house. Then Nicole came and kissed me on the mouth right in front of him. Then she turned, kissed him on the cheeks, and called him *Loulou*. He called her *Bébé*.

They opened French wine, and all the time Nicole is looking at me and smiling.

I would fuck them both, yelled Abou-Haddid. And the maid too.

Wait, listen. George stood up, filled with energy. Listen. Nicole takes off her shoes and plays footsie with me under the table. After dinner, the maid left the house.

I would fuck the maid, Abou-Haddid interrupted again. I would fuck the maid!

And we sat in the salon, George continued. She sat next to me and held my hand, right?

In front of her husband? Abou-Haddid asked.

Yeah, in front of him.

What did you do? I asked.

Well, I said, *Excusez-moi*, but are you really husband and wife?

Bien oui, said Laurent – that was the name of her husband. *Bien oui, George, absolument.* Nicole likes you. *C'est quoi le problème, alors?*

Nicole started to kiss me. Then she took my gun and she said, I love strong men. *Regarde, Laurent. Regarde, mon chéri*, and she handed him my gun, right? Laurent looked at it and said, *C'est un vrai guerrier, lui.* Now her hand was on my dick, right? She was breathing heavily, all excited. She went down on her knees, pulled my zipper down, and moved her head up and down.

In front of him? Abou-Haddid shouted. Do you believe this story, Bassam?

Wait, George interrupted. There is more. Now she is sucking me and the guy starts to cheer her on. He claps his hand and sings, *Vas-y, Nicole, vas-y, bébé, vas-y, bébé.* When I came, he ran to the kitchen, got her a towel, and held her face and cleaned around her mouth. All the time saying, *Bébé, mon petit bébé* . . .

Then Laurent asked me to leave. *C'est tard*, George, he said. *Nicole est fatiguée maintenant.*

He walked me to the door, thanked me, and said, Nicole likes you and we will call you again.

Did she call you? Abou-Haddid asked.

Yeah, she did.

Can I come with you? Abou-Haddid laughed. He bent toward the tray, his nose diving forward.

George walked me down the stairs on my way out and said, Listen, it seems tension is growing between you and Najib. You better work things out, or maybe both of you should stop the deal. I do not want Abou-Nahra to find out. If he does, he might ask me to put a bullet in both of your heads. If you need the money, you can always join the forces.

You talk to your cousin, I replied.

That night, through the flames of a million candles that brawled inside the neighbourhood houses, I walked. Under those lights, hazy behind nylon sheets that covered our broken windows, I walked the streets with no dogs. I walked, and the candles danced inside a city with injured walls, a city void of light, a broken city wrapped in plastic, and plastered with bullet holes.

On my way, I met Um-Dolly. She was going to the church for evening prayer, her head was covered in a black lace scarf.

I will pray for your lost soul, my son. God's wrath is great and it's upon us all.

God is dead, I said.

Um-Dolly shrieked and crossed herself, as if

101

she had just encountered the devil himself. I walked in the absence of the sun and I thought I saw the devil stalking me, sniffing like a nocturnal dog above barrels filled with bits of candles, fragments of journals, offal from slain goats, body refuse, rubble, ruins, shit, trash, human waste, house dreck, ship wreckage, broken glass.

I heard the engine of a car slowly ticking behind me. I looked back and saw the outline of three heads behind the windshield. In the dark I heard a man telling me to move onto the sidewalk. I looked back again and recognized Najib in the company of two men I had never seen before. Suddenly, they climbed out of the car, slammed the doors shut, and started to push me. I felt an elbow below my chin and a lock on my throat. One man held my hand and twisted it behind my back, and his companion pushed me onto the sidewalk. They cornered me against a metal door. Najib came up beside me and whispered in my ear, Don't show up at the machines anymore, do you understand? Don't even think about showing up. We will break your ugly face.

I tried to reach for my gun, but I was fighting for breath and my right hand was twisted up toward my shoulders.

You bring back what you stole from us, or my friends from the forces here will pay you a visit at your home, Najib whispered with an authority that clashed with his boyish voice. The two guys pulled back my arm and brought me down to the ground. I covered my head and curled like a worm under garden soil and waited for giants' soles to fall on me like gigantic leaves from high trees in titanic forests. I felt the men pounding on my ribs and on my face. Their feet followed their fists, raining down on my body like a winning jackpot. Najib spat on me and walked away.

I watched the three of them slamming their car doors and driving down toward Hospital Street. Then I bounced back like a demon: I ran with the drive of a thousand vengeful gods, salivating sweet blood and poisonous promises like a mad hyena, like metal piercing a beast's throat. I jumped over a fence and ran toward the alley that led me to Hospital Street (I, a lightning bolt of wrath, a Trojan horse's belly on fire, an erect cobra in an Indian valley). I jumped over another fence, landed on Hospital Street, and watched the car lights slowly moving toward me. I pulled out my gun, cranked it, and stood in the middle of the road. The car stopped and started to move backward in the narrow street. It smashed into parked cars left and right. I heard Najib squeaking, like a mouse in a lion's paw. I fired straight at the car and hit the right light. I moved to the side of the street near the wall, where it was darker. With both my hands extended, my finger on the trigger, I strolled slowly toward the car. Najib was howling, *Rja' ya Allah-rja*! (Go back, for God's sake, go back!). I fired another two shots at the car's left light. I saw the men's confused heads in silhouette, like trapped birds in a glass cage. I bled from my left hand, bit my swollen lip, ignored my tender ribs, and asked them to get out slowly. I said, Slowly. And, slowly. I said: Slowly.

Najib got out first. The other two put their arms up and moved toward me. I laid them all on the ground, on their bellies, in front of the car's fender, under a raging moon, parallel to my shoes and beneath my heavy breath, my dripping blood, and my shining devil's eyes. Najib croaked and cried like a hungry infant.

I frisked them; they had no weapons. I released Najib's two friends and ordered Najib to stay.

We took the car. I sat in the front seat. Najib drove. He cried all the way. He smelled of piss and his pants had a long patch of wetness that went down to his knees. He was crying and babbling and begging me as he followed my driving directions.

When we arrived under the bridge I asked him to get out. He clung to the steering wheel and started to move back and forth, sobbing, begging me not to kill him.

Get out, I said. I wouldn't hurt you. Just get out.

I am wet, he said. Tell me what you want.

Get out.

He opened the door slowly. Before he had a

chance to run, I grabbed him and pushed his waist over the warm hood and put the gun above his ear.

Who were the two guys with you?

I do not know them, he cried.

I know they are from the forces. Little Najib must know something. Who sent them?

Najib cried, and again he begged me not to kill him.

Okay, here is the deal. You talk, I won't kill. You do not talk, I will play Russian roulette with my automatic gun here. What are the chances, you think? Talk, or I will dump your body and expensive shoes in the sewer for the big rats to feed on. They would love to nibble on the French perfume behind your ears. *Ya chic inta.*

Najib shivered and a fresh, warm flood of piss came bursting through at his ankles.

Who are they? I said.

Najib cried, and protested that he had never met them before.

Okay then, to the rats!

No! No! Wait. They are De Niro's friends. Please do not tell him that I told you. I beg you on your mother's grave.

I am taking the car, I said. You walk home; it will dry you up.

I parked the car down the hill from Achrafieh and opened the glove compartment. It contained a flashlight and a paper. The paper was military authorization to pass the checkpoints. Najib's name was on it. I folded it and put it in my pocket.

I searched the rest of the car, but nothing else was there – no owner's papers, no weapons. I got out, shut the driver's-side door, and walked up the hill through the Syriacs' neighbourhood. A woman with a broom was chasing dust away from her doorstep and into the street. When I walked past, she stopped fanning the ground and took a long look at me. We stared at each other, then I walked on, and the rustles of her broom pondered and rose again.

The moon fell from above and hued the dancing laundry on the little roofs. Above, the heaven of the Christians was luminous with stars and the thin alleys were smeared with shadows.

I was breathing up through the hills, passing ground-floor windows. With quick, intrusive glances I extracted images of sepia photographs showing dead forefathers with remorseful faces, images of flamboyant vases with plastic flowers, of archaic sofas stained by old sins, of picturesque, romantic paintings of green valleys and brick-red houses, of massive, wooden dining tables with vampire chairs under crucifixes crucified on vertical walls. And I heard sounds, sounds of clanging pots, cutting knives, and ultraviolet radio waves that made dogs chase their tails. Outside in the backyards, laundry was hung by flabby arms and paraded on straight pins in army rows, like frescoes on Venetian balconies. I smelled boiling chicken broth, heard onion-scented hands tapping knives on cutting-boards in a crescendo like that of a castrated church-boys' choir, or of the soundless Aramaic tears that were shed, on that tempest day, for the nailed son of Yahweh and the dangled corpse of his companion, the forgiven thief.

George offered me a chair.

He pulled out his box of cigarettes, lit his fire, and threw the Marlboros on the table.

Is everything settled between you and Najib?

Before I had the chance to answer, he added: Forget about the poker machines. I have other work for you.

I kept my eye fixed on him. And no cigarette was lit between my fingers; only my throat burned, my eyes itched. Anger crawled down my chest and images from childhood bounced on the table: two boys pissing in the corner of angled walls, shooting doves with wooden guns, thieving candies with little hands, and swinging wooden sticks to herd car wheels down the city hills, wearing cheap open sandals, mouths pounding purple chewing gum, pockets bloated with marbles, chasing Indians and African lions with slingshots and crooked arrows, praying on bruised knees, confessing in foreign tongues while surrounded by flames that danced like our stolen cigarettes did at night in narrow alleys and under the stairs.

George lifted his glass. Whisky, he said.

Whisky, I whispered back sarcastically.

There is money in whisky. Work with me for a few months, forget about the poker place, make your money and leave.

I am not joining your military.

No, you do not have to. This is a side job. Cheap whisky from Romania, a few thousand imitation Johnny Walker bottles, and fake labels. You combine it all and you have Johnny ready to go. The manufacturer needs to send a few hundred cases of it to the Muslim side. You load a truck and meet someone downtown. You deliver, and that's it.

Who's in on the deal?

No one, just you and me and the manufacturer.

Abou-Nahra?

Abou-Nahra is not so important.

Are you coming along?

No. You do the delivery alone. I can get you a military pass, in case you're stopped. First you'll do it once a week. Give it a few weeks and the whole West Side will be begging for more.

It is an operation for two, I replied.

Well, who do you have in mind?

I will let you know.

Let me know soon. The first shipment has to

go on Thursday night, the man is waiting, and I thought of you first. I always think of you.

We all think of ourselves first and foremost, I said, and I threw him back his lighter and left.

CHAPTER 9

I leaned on the edge of my veranda and watched a few Christians go by. The faithful trotted past, like horses, carrying shopping bags; at the end of the street they lingered over vending carts that displayed kitchenware and vegetables. When the vendors called, housewives came out on their balconies and lynched baskets, money, ropes. They ordered by the dozen, negotiated from the sky, and handpicked goods while batting their long eyelashes. Their orders resonated against the broken walls. Their baskets came down from their verandas like buckets into dark wells. And when the vendor filled the baskets, these women, like miners, pulled on the ropes, started fires, and cooked meals in metal pots and red sauce.

I saw Rana walking by below. She dug her head toward the ground. She reached the end of the street and turned round and passed below me again. She was waiting for the housewives to fold up their ropes and their long tongues that entered every door, wrapped around every pillow, slithered like serpents in beds, and stretched under every young skirt to assess menstrual flows and hymens.

Tongues that slurp sauce on tasting spoons, I thought. Tongues that curse the dead, tongues that hang laundry and people's lives on balconies and roofs, tongues that tell . . .

My mother told me, Rana said, as she finally reached my door, either Bassam comes and asks for your hand or let him stop prowling like a cat around your window.

I am working on something, I said. Just be patient.

I cannot come here any more, Bassam. Abla, *haydi al-sarsarah*, saw me entering the building the other day, and she said the forty days of mourning are not over yet. In this neighbourhood, people watch and gossip all day. I am sick of it, Bassam, I am sick of the war and the people here. I want to leave, Bassam. Let's leave soon. You are not going to spend the rest of your life lifting boxes at the port.

I am working on something. Soon, I said. Soon we will leave, *khalas*. And I held her waist, kissed her lips, pulled her skirt up, and brushed my hand on her curves. Wetness and warmth streamed gently, warmth on fingertips, warmth on cracked lips, warmth from tongue on salty fingers, fingers spinning in curly hair, fingers splitting blouses, fingers crawling, fingers suffocating pillows.

We burned two cigarettes, and Rana said, I saw George the other day. He was driving a new BMW. Is it his?

Probably not. It must be Abou-Nahra's.

111

I was walking with my friend Leila the other day, said Rana, just talking and looking at clothes, and this nice sports car stopped next to us. I did not recognize George because he was wearing sunglasses. Then he pulled off his shades and asked us if we needed a ride. I said, No, thank you, we are not going too far. Then cars started to honk behind us and George's door was already open, so we got in. He drove us back here . . . He is so funny, he played this Arabic music very loud and drove like he was in a race . . . You're so quiet, Bassam . . . Your silence is breaking me, it is breaking me. All you want is to touch me. I meet you, and you want me to take off my clothes, and then you lie on your back and look at the ceiling, and smoke, and hardly say a word to me. You are breaking me.

Later, I went to George's place. Members of his platoon were stretched on his sofas, wearing cotton shirts, cowboy belts, and Levi's jeans. I recognized Nicole, the woman from Broumana. Her husband, Laurent, was drunk and talking about Africa. Highways of cocaine were stretched on mirrors. Noses operated on glass like vacuum-cleaner hoses, driving white powder into the molecules of numb, wide eyes. The apartment buzzed with invincible fighters, with swelling laughs and shiny teeth. The fighters filled the kitchen with their straight, broad shoulders, they sang to the music with commanding voices, they landed their lips and heroic praises on one another's cheeks, and their sharp-shooters' eyes were aimed on serpentine asses. There was food and drink and talk and cigarettes.

I stood against the wall with a beer in my hand. I talked to a few people: to Fadi, to Adel, to Raymond, to Souha, Chantal, Christine, Maya, Souhail, and to George, who was smiling and high.

George said, Have a good time now, and we will talk later. There is a girl inside bleeding from her nose.

I will ask one of your soldier friends, Joseph Chaiben, to help me with the whisky job, I said.

We will talk tomorrow, he said, and kissed me on the cheek. You're my brother, you're my brother, he said, and walked toward *Bébé* and her husband, Monsieur Laurent.

You came for the tea, the manufacturer said to me when he opened the door. Listen. It is simple. I make the contact. It is business; everyone drinks. Did you eat?

Yes, I said.

You have to try my wife's *bamia*. Come, sit down and eat.

No, I ate. Next time, thank you.

You like whisky? he asked me.

Only the good kind, I said.

The manufacturer laughed. I won't offer you any of mine, then. By the way, I knew your uncle.

He was always involved in politics. I would tell him, Stop wasting your time with all these activities. But he was a socialist, he liked demonstrations! At the warehouse tomorrow, my son Hakim will load the truck for you. You just give them the merchandise; no money exchange is involved. The contact's name is Ali. George gave you directions?

Yes, I said.

Will you be alone?

No.

It's just business, he said again. No religion, no war; this is only business. Muslim, Christian – it does not matter.

Joseph and I drove down to Al-Aswaq. The streets were vacant. Little plants sprang from beneath the sidewalk's cracks, lived underneath broken arches, shone in front of looted stores, sprang from the bellies of decaying sandbags, and dwelt in deserted governmental buildings that longed for the old days when lazy bureaucrats strolled in long hallways, snoozed on metal desks, dipped their moustaches in thick coffee, paraded their thin ties on hairy, conceited chests, waved their hands to expel flies and welcome bribes and seal endless deals with forged wills, illegal roofs, rebirth certificates, religious divorces, contaminated water pipes, underage driver licences, expired bank notes, stumbling constructions, derelict sewers, stained travel documents, and clandestine harvests of hallucinogenic plants that grew in the Bekaa Valley on the steps of Heliopolis, where Fairuz, that whining singer, sang at night under twinkling stars that had guided the three Babylonians from the east and down south into that stable with ruminating cows and the child who extracted milk from the virgin's round, black nipples.

I drove, and Joseph navigated. I know this place like my own fingers, he said to me. Turn right, there, next to the barrel. Stop.

I pulled out my gun, and got out of the van, and stood beside it. Joseph pulled out his AK-47 and took his position behind the vehicle.

Chai, come and get it. Chai, Joseph shouted.

A man whistled from the first floor of an empty building.

Ali? I asked.

Bassam?

Yes.

At Ali's signal, two young boys appeared from behind the sandbags. They were dressed in worn clothes and plastic flip-flops, and had dirt-smudged faces.

I got into the van and turned its rear toward the West Side of the city. The boys' tiny arms pulled cases from the van and carried them inside the building.

Forty cases, I said.

Mahmoud, did you count the number of cases?

Forty, the little kid shouted from inside the building. *Arba'in. Twakkalala Allah.*

Kassak, and watch out for the land mine on your way back, Joseph shouted to them.

Ten thousand needles had penetrated Nicole's arms, but still I brought her a little bag to open. Monsieur Laurent stood above the stove with a spoon in his hand, breaking powder and heating liquid.

Tiens, Bébé, mon amour. Tiens.

When the band around her arm was released, Nicole smiled at me. Should I give the money to George or to you?

Give it to George, I said.

I strolled down the stairs into the city, and over to the church walls, and under the church stairs I sat and smoked. A few cats with striped fur passed by, a few rifles meowed, a few heels licked the earth, and a few bells tolled on the roofs above me.

Eventually, George showed up with Abou-Haddid at his side.

How is the junkie? he asked me. Did the old man shoot as well?

No.

Did he pay you?

No, I told him to give you the money. You should have told me what was in the . . . I paused. Do you have the whisky cut for me?

The man did not pay me yet. When he pays I will take care of you, do not worry.

Next time, tell me what to expect. I am not your private pusher, I said. And I left.

George called out after me, but I did not answer him.

All the next day I lay in my bed and floated. Cigarette smoke hung about me, rose to the ceiling, and formed a grey cloud. Bombs fell in the distance. The plate under my bed was filled with ashes and yellow Marlboro butts with smashed faces and hunchback postures. The candle beside me shone its light on the comic book in my hand. My slippers waited for me under the bed like Milou, Tintin's dog. When I heard a knock at my door, I pulled my gun from under my pillow and killed the candle flame swiftly. I walked to the door in my slippers and glued my eye to the peephole. I saw a dark shadow.

I moved away from the door. Who is it? I asked.
It is me, Nabila. Bassam, open the door.
I obeyed.
Why are you hiding in the dark? Steal a candle from the priest, set the house on fire, but don't hide like a stray ghost.
Nabila followed me into my room. I swept the table with my hand, searching for the box of matches. When I found it, I shook it like a Brazilian musical instrument. I struck one stick against the box's rough edge, and Nabila's face shone.
You are still skinny, still yellow and skinny. Let me come tomorrow to cook for you and fix the house.

No, I said.

Have you seen Gargourty?

Yesterday.

I have not seen him in a week. I called his work-
place and they said he no longer works there. I
went many times to his place, but he is never home.
No one has seen him. Um-Adel, his neighbour,
said he is hardly ever home.

He must be busy.

Doing what?

Working.

At what?

I don't know. Whatever comes along.

Like what? What is he becoming? Is he working
with Abou-Nahra?

Yes.

But at what?

Security.

Security! Nabila shouted. Security for what? I
will call that fat slob Abou-Nahra. I will call him.
If a hair on my nephew's head is harmed, I will
curse his dead mother in her grave. Talk to George,
Bassam. He will listen to you. You two are
brothers. He should go to school.

I am leaving this country, I said.

Where to?

Rome, Paris, New York, wherever I can go.

Take him with you. Take him. Talk to him.
Yes, both of you leave. Go to France. I will give
you the name of George's father, that coward,
and ask him to send his son a French passport

and money. I'll ask him for George's papers, tell him that his son is lost. I'll tell him to invite George for a trip, for a vacation. May the virgin saint open all the good doors for you, Bassam. Help your brother. Help him. When do you leave?

I am waiting for some money to come.

I will give you money if you will just go and find George's father.

No, I will be all right.

Look at this house. Bassam! And Nabila picked up the glasses, the overflowing ashtrays, and the clothes from the floor.

Leave it, I said.

She continued picking up items and arranging them like my mother once had.

I grabbed her wrist, pulled a pillow from her hand, and threw it against the wall. Leave it, I said.

Nabila squeezed my hand and touched my face. Now that you're alone, you have to take care of yourself. Do not live in dirt like a rat. Open the window. This place smells of cigarettes and sweat. Look at you. Look at you now, unshaven, neglected.

She retrieved her hand, kissed me on the cheek, and walked out into the dark hallway and down to the street.

On our second delivery, Joseph and I had the van filled with sixty cases of Johnny Walker.

Joseph reached for a box, opened it, and pulled out a bottle.

Don't drink it. This shit might poison you. It is not a good day to die, I said.

No one dies before his time comes, said Joseph.

A fatalist fighter, I mocked him.

Listen, let me tell you this story, and we'll see if you believe in fate or not. We were at the *jabhah*. You know Youssef Asho? The Syriac boy? We call him RBG.

No.

Anyway, this kid was on duty one week. And I was in charge at the front that day. I see a woman, an old woman in black, walking toward us, you hear? I took the sniper gun and looked in the binoculars. I see a big cross on her chest, so I knew she was one of us. I called to her, *Ya khalti* (my aunty), where are you going?

She said she was there to see her son, Youssef. This woman must have walked through ten land mines and escaped them all. She appeared from nowhere, like a spirit.

I called Youssef. He was in the other building. Now, the fastest way for him to cross was over a little street, but that street is exposed to a sniper. The other way to cross is longer because one has to go around. When Youssef heard that his mother was there, he walked across the sniper's street, and on the last few metres a sniper bullet whizzed right above his ear and missed him.

When his mother saw him, she started to cry

and said that she had had a very ugly dream, and that her heart was telling her something horrible was going to happen.

Youssef was furious at her. He started to curse her, and he held her arm and pushed her, and shouted in her face, asking her to go back, calling her a crazy old woman.

I smacked him on his head, and told him to respect his mother, and never to talk to her that way. I ordered him to leave the *jabhah*. I do not want impolite people like you in my platoon, I said to him.

Then I made him take a jeep and drive his mother back home. Now, this guy gets home, takes off his clothes. His mother boils water for him, prepares the bathroom, and leaves. While he is cleaning himself, a bomb falls in the bathroom and kills him. It tore him to a million pieces. His mother became insane. Now she spends all her time living and praying on the steps of the Saydeh church. She took a vow, and ever since her son's death she has never bathed or cleaned herself. Now, what do you have to say to that story?

Drink, I said.

On the way to our drop-off with Ali in Al-Aswaq, Joseph and I encountered two young boys who stood in the middle of the street. They waved their hands at us. One of them had kinky hair and torn sneakers on his feet; the other was in jeans and open sandals. The one with the kinky hair held an AK-47, and the other had a gun stuck in his skinny waistband.

I stopped the van, opened the door, and walked toward them. Joseph followed me.

Stay in the van, one little kid shouted at me.

Who is in charge? Who is in charge here? I asked him.

I am, the boy said. Go back to the car.

I ignored his request and held my ground.

Where are the *shabab* going? the boy asked.

Why are you asking? Joseph said.

Open the back of the van and don't ask too many questions, the boy said.

Either you say who the fuck you are, or get out of the way! Joseph said.

The little kid took two steps back and with a little difficulty he cranked his rifle and pointed it at us. His friend ran over, shuffling his feet, wobbling under the weight of his gun, and pointed the weapon in Joseph's face. Open the van, the first kid shouted. Open the van! He pointed his machine at me. It looked twice his weight, and thrice his age.

Joseph and I walked toward the van. The boys rushed behind us.

The back door is locked. I have to get the key from the front, I said.

Both boys followed me as I opened the van. I pulled out the key with one hand, and with the other quickly reached for Joseph's military belt on the passenger's seat. I grabbed the first thing that stuck out of the belt – a hand grenade. Then I dropped the keys on the van's floor, dived under the wheel, squeezed my grip on the grenade spoon, and pulled the metal pin. I turned toward the kids and stretched my arm in their young faces.

Drop your weapons, *ya ikhwat al-sharmuta* (brothers of bitches), I said. I do not give a fuck about God or his happy kingdom. I will open my hand and we will all turn into pieces of meat.

Now, *ya wlad al-sharmuta*, that will teach you to fuck with the forces! Joseph shouted, and pulled out his gun and aimed it at their faces. Drop the shit from your hands, Joseph yelled. Count to three, Bassam. If they do not drop their weapons, open your palm. No one fucks with us!

The kid with the gun lowered his weapon first. The other held on to his AK-47 for a while. Then his eyes started blinking, and he began inhaling air through his nose at fast intervals. As soon as his *kalash* went lower in his hand, Joseph grabbed both weapons. He started to slap one boy while the other retreated slowly and then ran away through the back streets.

Joseph held the remaining kid by his T-shirt and swung him like bag of flour. He dragged him to the pavement and pounded him with his feet. *Ya kalb* (dog), who the fuck are you to stop us? he shouted.

The little kid started to cry, and hid his face in his skinny arms.

I am taking you to the cell to rot, *ya kalb*.

I walked to an empty building, tossed the hand grenade through a window, and plunged to the ground. It exploded and echoed through the whole world. Then I pulled Joseph away from the kid. The kid's little head was bleeding, and his nose was smashed. He lowered his eyes, swept the blood away with the back of his hand, and sobbed like the kid that he was.

Where are you from? I asked.

We live here in Al-Aswaq.

Why did you want to open the van? I asked.

We were looking for something to take, he said and spat blood.

To take where?

Something to sell, he said. We did not know that you are militiamen.

Where did you get your weapons?

We took them from a dead Syrian soldier.

How old are you? I demanded.

Fourteen.

What's your name?

Hassan, he said.

Fucking Muslims in our district, Joseph shouted and pulled out his gun. Let me finish this dirt!

I held Joseph's arm and pushed him into the van.

When I looked back I saw the kid escaping, limping through the bombed city's walls.

Back in the van, Joseph laughed and called me *Majnun*.

We are going to call you *Al-Majnun*, he said.

You could have killed us all with that Russian grenade. It is the worst kind you can choose to open, because it is the most unpredictable; it might take a second or it might take three minutes to explode, and both ways we would have been finished. *Majnun*. He started to laugh louder . . . *Majnun*.

When we arrived at our drop-off, Ali and his boys were waiting for us. While the boys emptied the van, Ali walked toward me and offered me a cigarette.

How are things on the other side? I asked.

Once it was all one side, but now we call it the other side, Ali said and shook his head. Have you ever been to the other side? he asked me.

Long time ago, when I was young. I have a relative on the other side.

Oh yes?

Yes, a communist uncle.

What is his name?

Naeem Al-Abyad.

I know your uncle, said Ali, surprised. We fought together. He is a high commander in the communist party now. Do you two ever communicate?

No, not for a long time.

I saw Joseph approaching us. I winked to Ali, and we changed subjects.

When the boys finished moving the whisky, I told Joseph that I needed to take a piss. I walked behind a wall and called to Ali.

Can you find a way to tell my uncle that my mother is dead? I asked him.

Allah yirhamba (may she rest in peace), he said and lowered his head. I will get in touch with your uncle.

CHAPTER 10

I woke to the sound of knocking in the middle of the night. When I opened my apartment door, I saw Monsieur Laurent standing in the hallway with a candle in his hands. I invited him in.

I am looking for George, he said.

Did you check his house?

Yes, and he is not there.

Maybe he is on duty, I suggested.

Where? It is urgent.

Check the *sakanah* (army barricade). Or maybe he went on a mission. He mentioned something about it last week at his party.

We need another fix for Bébé. She is shivering.

I cannot help you, Monsieur Laurent.

It is urgent.

Why don't you take her to a rehab place?

Yes, I am waiting for a vacancy at the clinic in France . . . A blood change. They do blood changes.

Monsieur Laurent, why do you do this?

Why do I give Bébé everything?

Why do you let her do anything she wants?

Can I have a cigarette?

Yes. Do you want some coffee?

No. But let me answer your question. You see, once, we Lebanese ruled Africa. We were the middlemen. We extracted commissions left and right. We built that place. When I left my native village and took a boat to meet my French uncle in Africa, neither you nor Bébé were even born yet. And all I wanted was to save money, work with my uncle for a while, and come back to the village, to that hill, and build a house and get married to a decent local girl.

But the community got rich. We worked in slums and jungles selling textiles. We became the middlemen for the French, and the Portuguese, and whoever else came. We brought cars and electric fridges to the place, we bribed the policemen, the mayors, the army generals, and we all lived in penthouses. Do you know that all the Lebanese in Africa lived in penthouses?

We threw parties in our private clubs. As a young man I worked hard and learned how to buy and sell. I travelled with suitcases filled with bills that smelled of African soil and humid mattresses. We swallowed stones in African bathrooms and walked into Swiss hotels and defecated diamonds. We had mulatto women under our feet, dancing on our tables to Arabic songs that made us decadent and nostalgic. You see, the Lebanese ruled these places without guns, without an army, without slaves.

But then the time passed. And that little hill where I left a virgin bride kneeling in a church pew until her thighs wrinkled and her knees turned to soap – all those years, that little hill stayed on my mind. You see, I, too, lost and gained, and took private planes, and bet on blackjack tables until the gamblers' nails tore the green table's lawn . . . We worked those corrupt generals, we had them in the palms of our hands.

We sucked the locals' wealth, and offered their daughters as gifts. You see, no one liked us, but they all needed us. And then it happened, that day when the poor walked barefoot into the city, with guns and machetes in their hands, and chased us out of our penthouses. They stumbled over our long chairs, defecated in our mosaic pools, snapped our *argilahs* (pipes) in half, camped in our marbled saloons with large windows that looked over their primitive villages, their shanty towns that we never noticed, their running sewage that we never smelled, their chocolate-skinned sisters whose bellies we used as pillows, whose pale palms we used as towels for our Semitic semen, for our sweating foreheads behind circled walls and guardian dogs.

So I escaped, leaving behind my resorts that once shone with Europeans' and Afrikaners' red-burned skins. I left the cars, the soap factory, my mixed-race, illegitimate descendants. I ran and came back here, looking for that virgin, looking for that childhood hill.

I am an old man now, so forgive my sentimentality. When I met Bébé she was alone. I met Bébé on the top of a hill, and I took it as a good omen. I bought her everything she needed, everything she asked for. Why? you ask. I am afraid I have nothing else to offer her, and now she is a home, a daughter, and a wife. Forgive my tears, but I am afraid that she might ask me if we can leave this place. And all I am trying to do is to spend my last days close to that hill.

Now, could you seek George for me? *S'il vous plait.*

The next day, I walked through the neighbourhood. I entered a grocery store.

We have fresh green almonds, the grocer, Julia, said to me. Good for a *kass*! Do you want a kilo?

No, I'm not drinking much these days.

Do you have any empty bottles to return? I will send my daughter Souad to get them.

I am not sure. I will look in my mother's kitchen.

Allah yirhamha, your mother was a lady. May God cut their hands . . .

I bought some bread and *labnah*, thanked Julia, and left.

On the way back, I came across a jeep driving the wrong way. It was packed with young militiamen in green suits, and with bands wrapped around their foreheads, who pointed their rifles toward balconies and the French *abat-jours*. The jeep pulled up next to me, and George got out of it. He looked tired and dirty.

We just got back, Bassam, he said. Ten days without a shower. We ate canned food, and my boots are cutting the back of my ankle. Akram Seiff, you know him? We call him Alnasek, the brother of Jean Seiff.

Yes, he lives above Antoun's Laundromat, I said.

He got hit under the arm, and he bled to death. There are fucking black Somalis fighting with those Palestinians. Did you know that? The whole *'ummah* is here fighting us.

We walked toward my house. George's boots were rimmed with brown soil, and his beard had grown in with straight black hair. He lifted his Kalashnikov and manoeuvred with difficulty through the cars that jammed our narrow streets; he was like an American soldier with his arms above his head, advancing slowly and half-immersed through the swamps of Vietnam. On the way, we stopped at the grocer's and picked up a few green bottles of Heineken. We took the stairs up to my apartment, because in Beirut, that crowded city, the electricity came and went as it pleased. Hardly anyone used the elevators any more, and those who did risked getting stuck and spending hours in small mechanical boxes that hung from metal ropes as old and decayed as the last French soldier who left this place.

George dumped his gear and rifle on the chair

in my living room. He took off his boots and lay down on the sofa.

Where did Al-Nasik die? I asked.

In Kfar Al-Wali.

How?

Open the beer and sit down. It is a long story. Are you going somewhere?

No, not yet, I replied. I opened two bottles of beer and extended one toward his chest.

No work at the port today?

Yes, but there is still some time before I go. Speak, I said, I am listening.

George took a long first sip and stretched out on the seat. He said: Warm beer. He paused, and then he talked without stopping, and I did not interrupt him.

Around four in the morning I heard some shots coming from the next village, George began. I woke up, and woke the platoon. It was freezing, with that morning mountain cold. We arrived at the village around four-thirty, maybe five. Hanfoun, the commander, was on leave. I was second in command. I split the platoon; I sent Joseph (your partner, he added, with a wink) and Alakhtabout to hold a position up the hill. We parked the jeeps at a distance, turned off the headlights, and went on foot. We moved toward the village main street. I asked Abou-Haddid to come with me, and we ran ahead of the platoon. When the day started to break, we could see more clearly. I saw a few women and kids exiting from the back of an

132

unfinished concrete builiding. They were rushing down toward the valley. They carried plastic bags and wool blankets. We ran toward them. I asked them where they were going. The eldest among them, a woman with a black headscarf, told us, We are going down. Where down? I asked, snatching one of her bags, throwing it on the ground, and prodding it with my boots. They were all trembling with fear. One of the kids started to cry quietly.

I asked the woman, Where are the men?

She was silent for a moment. Then she said that she and her companions did not live here, that they were refugees looking for a place to stay but had been kicked out of the building this morning.

Who is in the building? Who kicked you out?

Men.

What men? I asked.

She fell silent again.

How many?

Two, she mumbled.

I said, Go walk, and don't say a word or look behind you. If one of you gives a sign, I will aim at the kids first.

The women grabbed the children and rushed down into the valley, slipping and falling down the hills. All the women were in black for mourning, so I figured they must have been all related. I asked Abou-Haddid to go back and give a sign to the rest of our guys to advance.

As soon as Abou-Haddid walked back, pressing himself against the edge of a stone wall, bullets showered on him from the top of the building. He dug into an irrigation canal that crept all around the village. The water must have been freezing. When they heard the shots, the rest of the guys rushed toward us and started to fire back at the building. I was left alone under the building, you see? I was thinking: I'll take the stairs, and engage the two men upstairs, and finish them off. But I had no sign from Abou-Haddid. I was waiting for the firing to cease so I could cross and see if he was still alive. But I tell you, this Christian man is like a frog. He slid into the water and disappeared. The whole thing was a set-up. You see, while the two men in the building got our attention, an enemy jeep was advancing from behind the platoon. A classic ambush, right? The two men in the building were planted to distract us. The only thing that saved us was that Joseph and Alakhtabout were rushing down from the hill and saw the jeep coming behind us. They engaged the men in the jeep and it was enough to warn the others. I knew something was not right when I heard fire from a different direction. I sensed it was an ambush.

Meanwhile, Abou-Haddid crawled in the canal and, like a wet rat, showed up on the other side of the building. He was shivering with cold. He took off his shirt and I gave him my jacket. Then we decided to go up to the building and finish the two men, and then go back and join the platoon. I went up first, in case Abou-Haddid's machine gun was too soaked to fire. But, you know, the Kalashnikov is rugged; water or dust does not affect it. Fuck the M-16. It feels like a toy. An AK-47 is still the best, I tell you. That is why I switched rifles myself. Even Israelis wanted us to trade AK-47s with them.

It was hard to locate exactly where the firing was coming from because every shot echoed through the empty concrete. But we knew there were only two men, right? So Abou-Haddid and I waited. Then, when the fire intensified, we rushed up the stairs so they couldn't hear us coming. When we got to the third floor, I heard one of the shooters changing his magazines. I opened a *rummanah* (a hand grenade) and threw it inside the room, and we both dug down behind the wall. The fucking explosion was so loud it made our ears whistle for days. They still do now, and sometimes I still get a strong headache and ringing in my ear. The building was under construction, so the dust blew and wouldn't settle. Not only were we deaf, we were blind: We were lost in a thick cloud of dust, and dust filled our breathing. We became deaf, blind, and breathed with difficulty. Still, we had to get up and comb the room to make sure there were no survivors. Abou-Haddid started to shoot in the direction of the room. I started to shoot as well, but there was nothing. Abou-Haddid said he saw a shadow, but it must have been the effect of his wet, cold testicles that made him see things.

As George said this, he laughed, and I laughed too. Then he continued.

The two men were already on the floor. After we combed the room with shots, I could hear that one of them was still almost breathing. I looked at his face and I saw a Somali or African of some kind, right? I stuck him with my bayonet and finished him right away. They are coming from all over the world to fight us, Bassam, here in our land. Palestinians, Somalis, and Syrians – everyone has a claim on this land, right?

Abou-Haddid and I rushed back to join the platoon. By that time, Elnasek, who was positioned in the back and closer to the jeeps, was already hit under his arm. I tell you, this guy was wounded and still he held off the enemy for about fifteen minutes. We covered for Zaghlloul, who rushed and pulled Elnasek back. We tried to get to the jeeps, but the enemy forces held the road. Elnasek was still bleeding. I think he could have been saved if we had got him to a hospital on time, but the other side held us for a few hours before we had some reinforcement. Only then could we engage them and make them retreat. So Elnasek bled to death. Before he lost consciousness, he held the *zakhirah* and an icon of Saint Elias that he always had wrapped round his arm with a rubber band. We detached the icon and gave it to him, and he kissed it and started to pray.

Then a few minutes later he went unconscious, and he died in Zaghlloul's arms. He was a pious man.

Here George paused. Then he asked, Is the water running?

You can go check. By the way, Nabila is asking for you, I said.

Yeah?

And Monsieur Laurent is asking for you as well.

I know what the old man wants; he did not pay for Nicole's last fix yet.

What the fuck are you doing, George, hooking that girl?

That impotent is loaded. He has African diamonds up his ass, George said.

He went to the bathroom, poured water in a bucket, washed his hands, splashed water on his face, and then he took off his socks, examined the blisters around his ankles, and poured the rest of the water on his feet. He borrowed some of my clothes and lay down on my sofa.

George and I ate together that day. I smoked a cigarette to help me digest the food I ate with him.

After the meal, I left the fighter asleep and drove his motorcycle to the port. I worked all night. At the dock, the sea breeze splashed against my sweat. I drove the loading machine in the salty wind, lifted its arm, and stocked merchandise inside warehouses.

In the morning, at the end of the shift, I walked

to the office of Abou-Tariq, the foreman. Each morning, a few men gathered in front of Abou-Tariq's container. His container was transformed into an office, and we all sat on plastic chairs and empty ammunition boxes in front of it, sipping coffee and talking. Abou-Tariq was an old combatant who had fought in the battle of Tal-Alzatar, and who prided himself on knowing the high commander, Al-Rayess, personally. He played with his moustache and informed us that a large ship was arriving next week.

We need more men to unload, Abou-Tariq said. He suggested that the security men should go to Dawra and pick up Egyptian or Ceylonese workers to help with the unloading.

Chahine, a young security man with a thin face and a dark complexion, chain-smoked with an air of boredom. Now he stood up, lit yet another cigarette, and said in a low, quiet voice, These poor workers stand in the sun all day waiting for an employer to hire them for construction work and other manual jobs. But now, when they see our militia jeeps coming their way, they start running. They do not want to work for free. Sometimes the forces even forget to feed them. The last time we needed workers, I had to run after an Egyptian from Dawra to Burj Hammoud. I tell you, this guy had plastic slippers, but he ran like a gazelle. Finally, I was out of breath, so I stopped, took my gun, and started to shoot in the air. He thought I was shooting at him, so he stopped. I dragged him to the jeep and we drove up to the mountains. We needed men to fill sandbags for a new military position we held. It was April, and was warm down here in the coast, but when we got high up into the mountains it was cold, especially at night. These workers were in short sleeves and without shoes or jackets. They huddled next to one another in the back of the jeep. We made them fill sandbags, then in the evening the temperature dropped even more. In the morning, we found one of them frozen to death. His friends were all crying. One of them was in tears next to his friend's dead body. Chakir Ltaif, nicknamed Beretta, approached the fellow and asked him for a cigarette. The man stopped crying, and he looked Beretta in the eyes, and said, *Danta, ya beh, mush ayiz iddik cravata harir kaman?* (Your highness, do you want me to offer you a silk tie as well)? I tell you, since that day, I refuse to force these people, or run after them or capture them. They have a *ruh* (spirit) as well. I will not do it, *khalas.*

Said, another man who worked at the port – he was in charge of the merchandise inventory and accounting – looked at Chahine and said, Well, I want to see how they will treat you in Egypt if you go to work there. You are a Christian. Look at the Copts and other Christians. How are they treated in these Muslim countries?

I am not sure why I opened my mouth – me, who wanted only to finish my sip of coffee, crush my cigarette on the floor, and board a ship to nowhere. To my own surprise, I said, There are many Christians on the West Side of Beirut, still living there, and no Muslim ever bothered them.

They are all traitors, communists, and socialists, Said quickly replied. And maybe you two should join them, he said, and looked at me and Chahine with hateful eyes.

Who are you calling communist, you thief? We all know what you do, Chahine protested, and his gun tilted slightly up toward the edge of his chest. My brother is a *shahid* (martyr). My brother died fighting for the cause. My brother threw himself on a hand grenade to save his platoon.

Yeah, we have heard that story many times, Said replied. But we also all know that it was your brother's fault. He opened that grenade and couldn't throw it, so it fell at his feet. He was clumsy, that is all; everyone claims to be a hero in this war.

Ars (pimp), I am going to kill you, Chahine shouted. He cranked his AK-47, but before he had the chance to aim it at Said, Abou-Tariq grabbed the rifle, pushed it high toward the sky, and started to slap Chahine on the face, telling him to release his weapon.

When the young man obeyed, Abou-Tariq declared: No one raises a weapon toward anyone in my presence or here on my turf. Next time a gun is raised, no matter what direction it is aimed at, it is as if it is pointed at me personally, and I will deal with it. He shouted at all of us and told us to disperse.

As I walked toward the motorcycle, Said drove by me slowly in his beaten-up Mercedes. He stared at me, and I looked back at him.

What was your last name again? he asked me.

I did not answer him, and did not take my eyes off his car window. I remained calm because I could see that both his hands were on the streering wheel.

Said nodded his head slowly, then one of his hands moved and dangled out of the car widow. Yeah, Al-Abyad, I just remembered, he said with sarcasm. There are a few of those names still living on the other side, I bet. He drove away.

I hopped on the motorcycle and drove home. As I reached my street, from the corner of my eye I saw Rana leaving my building. I saw George leaving behind her, heading in a different direction. She looked back at him and fixed her hair. Then she gave him a sign with her hand, and ducked her head into her shoulders, and slipped away fast, brushing against corners and the clandestine walls.

When I saw them, I made a sharp turn and took Saydaleh Street. I drove through Achrafieh; I drove fast, racing and cutting in front of cars. Four young men in a red Renault decided to race me. They jeered at me and honked behind me, and tried to block my way. One of them stretched his upper body from the back window of the car while his friend held him from the waist. He extended his hands and tried to catch me to bring me down. I accelerated, climbed on the sidewalk, stomped one foot on the ground, leaned the machine toward the curb, and gave it gas. It swung in the opposite direction, and I drove the wrong way up the street and lost them.

I went back to my house. The dishes were clean.

I slept all morning. In the afternoon I walked toward Rana's house. I waited across from her building, pacing, with a cigarette in my hand. I leaned against the wall of the fish store. I waited, and it rained and poured, and the water rushed down from the roof and peed its way through pipes and drains, splashing on sidewalks. Faces sunk beneath colourful umbrellas passed me by. Cars made their way through little pools and drove wedges through the water, splashing it into ephemeral, flying waves.

Then the old sun came out again, and the roofs, like wet dogs, shook the rain from their backs, and the fisherman's fish had a last bounce, shedding its freshness, forgetting its home under the sea. I waited for Rana, but she never came down to dip her feet in the wet streets.

★   ★   ★

Then next day I arranged to meet Rana at my house. I asked her why she never came by any more.

I have been busy, she said.

You never passed by?

Busy, I have been busy. She looked away, confused.

Should I thank you for doing the dishes? I asked, seizing Rana by the hair, pulling her head back, and kissing her neck violently, fumbling at her breasts.

Bassam! she whispered, sounding scared and bewildered. I pulled her by her dress to my parents' room, ripping her clothes, snapping the buttons on her blouse. She attacked me with her nails. I slapped her face. She cried, escaped me, and ran out of the room with a naked breast, stumbling over chairs and hitting the wall arches. She threw herself on the doorknob, twisting it as if the house was on fire, and staggered out.

I went to my parents' room and looked in the mirror. Tears slipped out of my eyes. I opened the drawer, grabbed my father's handkerchief, and wiped my face with it.

Then I loaded my gun and walked toward George's place. I banged on his door, but no one answered.

I took his motorcycle and drove fast up to the mountains and into the empty hills. I parked at the top of a cliff. I looked down at the green, and watched and cursed the brown valleys that were covered with listless patches of soil. I pulled out my gun and shot at the hills, and at the birds, and the echoes of my shots bounced on stones, and lamented and boomeranged treacherous syllables back to me.

CHAPTER 11

A few days passed and ten thousand Johnny Walkers marched west, burning throats and breaking houses. Men drank liquor, and bedroom doors slammed, and thighs closed with promises never to reopen, and rings were pulled from fingers and tossed toward old dressers, weeping mirrors, and joining walls.

One afternoon I received a call from the whisky manufacturer. He asked me to do an urgent delivery for the next day.

The next morning I picked up the whisky from the warehouse. Then I passed by Joseph's place and picked him up. In the van, I handed Joseph some money. He counted it and smiled.

Ali was late for his delivery, so we waited. Soon, one of the kids showed up and informed us that Ali was on his way. I asked Joseph to back up the van. Then I walked behind the wall and met Ali. He shook my hand, opened his jacket, pulled out an envelope, folded it in two, and quickly slipped it inside my jacket. He winked at me. I waited until Joseph was far from the van, watching the kids unload, then I quickly hid the envelope under the van's seat.

On the way back to our neighbourhood, Joseph mentioned that he had seen a few Israelis on the street recently. They are coming, he said. Give it a month or so, and you will see them here, chasing out the Syrians and the Palestinians.

How do you know?

De Niro came by to see me the other day, said Joseph. He told me that he needed me for a security operation. He picked up a few other trusted men, and we drove to the mountains. When we arrived, they told us that Al-Rayess was there for a meeting with an important Israeli general. So we cleared and surrounded the whole area. Half an hour later, a helicopter landed and five Israeli military men came down. They all had burgundy boots: Special Forces. They held a three-hour meeting with Al-Rayess. Your friend De Niro is a big shot now, the right hand of Abou-Nahra.

What is the Israeli general's name? I asked.

General Drorir something . . . I can't remember.

When I arrived home I rushed to my room and opened the envelope from Ali. It was a letter from my Uncle Naeem:

Dearest Bassam,

I learned of your mother's death with great sadness. It brought tears to my eyes, and it even made me sadder not to be able to attend the funeral. I long to be with you, especially in these hard times. I often wonder what your life is like on the East Side alone, and orphaned at such a young age. I did not attempt to get in touch with you or your mother all these years for fear that my position with the leftist forces might put you and your mother in jeopardy. But you are welcome to cross to West Beirut any time. I can arrange for your coming here. You can stay with me, my wife, Nahla, and your cousin, Nidal, whom you have never met. I have sent you this small amount of money, in case you might be in need. I have also enclosed another envelope to be delivered to an old acquaintance of mine by the name of Jallil Al-Tahouneh. Enclosed is his contact information. He is expecting your call.

I send you all my love.
Your uncle who misses you,
Naeem

I copied down the name and the number of my uncle's contact, tore the letter to pieces, burned it in an ashtray, and counted the money. There were ten hundred-dollar bills, new blue bills that almost whistled. The other envelope from my uncle was closed and bore the initials J.T., for Jallil Al-Tahouneh. I opened it. There was a bundle of money and what looked like a map, or architectural drawings of a house foundation. The word *asas* (foundation) was written in red and circled on some areas of the map.

That night, I wanted to avenge a wrong done to me. I stood across from the poker place and waited. I saw Najib's friend leaving. I watched him from across the street. I saw that he drove an old, beaten-up blue car.

I put on my helmet and hopped on the motorcycle and followed him to Dawra.

In Dawra, I waited until he parked his car. He went inside a baker's store and came out with a *lahm ba'ajin* in his hand. He unwrapped the newspaper around his food and took a few bites, then walked to his apartment. When he entered the building I followed him up the stairs. As he arrived on the landing between two floors, I grabbed him from behind and twisted his shoulder, and once his face was exposed to me I hit him with my head (I was still wearing the helmet that, I hoped, would make me appear to him like a spaceman from a B movie). He fell on the stairs and moaned, his hands on his bleeding nose, his eyes bloodshot. I searched his pockets, pulled out money, put it in my jacket, and walked away and around the block. I found my motorcycle and drove it back home.

When night came again, like it always does, I dressed in black and smudged my face and hands with black shoeshine liquid. I lit a candle in the window on the street side of my apartment and

148

locked my door. I wore a hat that covered my curly hair, a hat long enough to hide my wide eyes, a hat that concealed me from nights, birds, and the grocer's eyes. I crossed the street to the building opposite. All is in opposition, I thought: cities, guns, friends, and foes. I went straight up to the building's roof. Slowly and calmly I opened the heavy metal door, gently closed it behind me, walked to the edge of the roof, and sat and eyed the street below. I watched the light that shone and danced in my window.

A car drove by once, slowly, then came back again, turned off its headlights, and stopped in front of my house. I rushed down the stairs with my gun in my hand. I hid in the entrance and watched Najib and his accomplice, who had a bandage on his puffy blue face and wrapped around his broken nose. They looked toward my window. They appeared childish, clumsy, scared, hesitant. I stood there, like a vindictive ghost in a squeaky attic restraining his accusing finger from pulling the trigger, restraining himself from reaching an invisible arm inside his enemies' throats to extract their last breaths. Najib and his friend whispered to each other, and then suddenly they drove away and did not return.

I went back to the roof and thought of George. I had almost killed George, my childhood friend, my brother who stabbed me and kissed me, and who kissed my lover long enough to leave me . . . I have to leave this place, I thought; I have to leave

149

this place. I pulled all my money from my pocket, and counted it again, and wrapped elastic around it to make a round, fat bundle.

I walked to the other side of the roof and watched Rana's house. Her window was dark. I swung the gun around in every direction, waving it at the vacant water-barrels, the dancing partridge bird, the whistling bombs, waving it in Rana's direction and in mine. I looked the gun in the face and I thought of the many ways to leave: The ghost could twist your arm and squeeze the trigger in your face, and if you're lucky, my friend, he will push you over the roof and wait for the partridge bird to carry you back up, and he will chase the falling rockets back to the Nevada desert, or to the ticking Big Ben, or to the bent Pisa tower. Or you might hold the cooing partridge tight, and dive into the sea, and hunt for poison fish and a few snapping clams. Or you might gracefully catch a cruise ship by its sails and swing it to its own mambo tune, careful not to spill champagne on the tourists' evening gowns while shooting water guns on migrating, sexless Byzantine angels. Or you might well trap sailors' ghosts in water bubbles, and watch them burst on the surface, and drown them again. Or you might slay underwater nymphs, collect their tiny green jackets, roll them like grape leaves, like the money in your pocket, like Persian carpets aired on white balconies.

Or you might just walk down the empty stairs, back to your flickering candle, and get some sleep.

★   ★   ★

In the morning, I heard a knock at my door. It was Monsieur Laurent. He looked distressed, and his eyes were red.

Your friend George came to visit me last night and acted like an animal, Monsieur Laurent told me. He wanted more money. I gave him what I usually give him, but he said that he wanted more. Then he took Bébé by the hand and left, and they have not come back since. He was hostile, very hostile. Could you look for him, please? I couldn't sleep all night.

Monsieur Laurent, I said, I am not George's agent. George asked me to do him a favour the other night when I brought you what you needed. If I had known what it was all about, I wouldn't have delivered the bag to you.

George was very hostile, Monsieur Bassam, pleaded Laurent. I even think he was a little high. He is asking for a lot of money now. He threatened me. *Il faut qu'on quitte cet endroit. C'est* devenu vraiment dangereux ici. I guess this is my destiny to be an exile, always an exile. Could you please look for George and Bébé? I just want to see *mon Bébé*.

Did you check George's house, Monsieur Laurent?

No. I am afraid your friend might get angry. *C'est un fou. S'il te plait*, go look for them.

I asked Monsieur Laurent to have a seat while I went inside to change. I brushed my teeth and splashed my face with a handful of water. I walked to the bedroom and put my pants and shirt on.

151

On my way out to the living room I held my jacket with my finger and slipped my hand in the jacket's sleeve. Monsieur Laurent held the second shoulder and helped with the other sleeve.

I walked out of the apartment and down the street, and Monsieur Laurent followed me. Then he rushed to walk beside me. Abou-Dolly, the grocer, passed us. He ignored me, but turned his face to Monsieur Laurent, and they both nodded politely to each other.

At George's place, I knocked on the door. Laurent stayed down by the entrance, pacing with his cigarette, coughing an old man's cough.

I banged on the door again. Finally Bébé opened it, half-naked, half-asleep.

Is George here?

Non, il n'est pas là.

Where is he?

He left.

Your husband is downstairs looking for you.

Ah, oui! Loulou est là? Barefoot, she rushed down the stairs.

When Laurent saw his wife, he coughed some more, threw the cigarette on the pavement, and walked toward her.

Bébé, Bébé.

Mais, ça va, mon amour, ça va, Nicole said, and she caressed Laurent's blond hair.

J'ai pas dormi.

Oui, mais ça va. Nicole held his hand and kissed his cheeks.

While the two of them were downstairs talking, I entered George's home and went to his room. Beside the bed, there was a thin needle and a burnt spoon; his rifle was lying in the corner. The place smelled of fumes and medicine. A lace bra was on the floor. I walked to the kitchen; the dishes were dirty and filling the sink. I glued my lips to the faucet; the water was weak, about to die and become extinct. I ran the last drops down my throat. They tasted of the air in the pipes.

I went back down the stairs. Bébé was rushing up, into George's house.

Je viens, papa, je serai là dans cinq minutes, j'apporte mes affaires.

Downstairs, Laurent held my hand and tried to kiss it. I pulled it away fast.

Merci, merci, he repeated like a servant as I walked past him. When I reached the sidewalk, I stepped on Monsieur Laurent's cigarette and put out its fire.

On my way home, I passed by Romanoce, the magazine store owner, and picked up a newspaper. The headlines: *Israel moving on the southern borders. Fighting in the mountains between the Christians forces, the Muslims, and the socialist forces. Long, empty speeches by ministers and clergymen. A model or Hollywood actress marries a Saudi millionaire. Woody Allen plays the clarinet. Saheeb Hamemeh declares his love to an Egyptian actress.* Meanwhile, Romanoce wondered if I would ever buy the newspaper, or would read it and put it back on the rack like I usually did.

Back on the street, Abou-Youssef stopped me and gave his condolences for the death of my mother. Salah, the plumber, saw us, paused apologetically, and said to me: May God rest her soul, two days before she died I fixed the pipes in your kitchen. My wrench and a few tools are still lying under your sink, and there is a small bill that maybe you can settle. I know it is not the time to ask, but the kids are without clothes, the wife is cursing the day she married me and her tyrant father who forced me on her, and my thick hands that are covered with calluses, and my chopped-up index finger that will never touch her saggy breasts again. She curses her fate. So this is me asking you for the rest . . . And may God rest your mother's soul. Such a lady.

I walked back home with Salah, and opened the door to him, and he went straight to his tools. I ducked behind the dining-room table and took my bundle of money from my pocket. I pulled out a few bills, straightened up, and gave Salah what my mother owed him.

When I returned to the street, it was calm. For the last few days, bombs had not flown our way. Taxi drivers fought over gas, women cursed the saints of cascades and water, and the men looked defeated in their unshaven beards. A few of the men showed off old guns that hung around their waists. People buzzed between stores, and card players disappeared like Houdini inside cafés obscured by a thick haze of *argilahs* smoke. The tobacco-apple aroma covered the garbage smells, and shielded the gamblers from the wrath of their hysterical wives.

As I walked, I passed my old school. Children in grey smocks walked in groups, books in their hands and in their brown satchels. They shuffled their feet in the direction of the long refectory, toward the priest in long robes, toward Napoleonic battles, toward ninety-degree triangles, toward *Jahiliyyah* poems of drunken Bedouins who praised many gods, and mourned the dead who dwelt under soft sand, over the shifting dunes, swaying with the dancing palms under a little bowl of half-lit moons.

CHAPTER 12

Israeli soldiers entered our land, splitting rivers and olive trees.

Vartan and I were reading the newspaper on the edge of the sidewalk. The headlines blared: *The Jews are in the south! The Syrians have pulled back! The Muqawamah is getting ready! The Christian forces are allying themselves with the invaders!*

Abou-Fouad passed by, and stuck his head into our open paper, and whispered, They are here. I heard the radio. We will get rid of those Palestinians, and be stuck with the Israelis.

Al-Chami, the street-corner musician, played with his *beats* and passed his hand over his moustache. Whoever comes, let him come. We are tired of this war, he chanted. We need to work, and the grey partridge on the roof will coo in my head when are we departing, when are we departing. Let's catch the southern wind. I can glide! I can glide across the nearby sea.

On my way back home, I met Monsieur Laurent. He held my arm, nodded, and said, *Les Juifs sont là, ils sont là.*

★   ★   ★

I saw Rana once in the market; she ignored me and slipped away through the merchants' calls. I followed her. When I approached her, she pretended not to see me and continued picking vegetables.

I took her hand and said, Come, let's talk.

She softly answered, We have nothing to say to each other. Please, take your hand off me. Go. Leave. You always wanted to be alone; all you wanted is to leave. You do not need me; you do not need anyone. Besides, I am getting engaged. And do not ask, I will never tell you to whom.

I will find out and kill your fiancé, I said.

You can try. My fiancé has killed many before you, and will kill many more.

I let her go.

The loud radio next door announced to me that the Israelis had moved north and laid siege on West Beirut.

From my balcony I watched the Christian forces, euphoric, driving their jeeps in haste. They had flamboyant orange flags pasted on their roofs, attached to their windows, on their hoods. When I asked Joseph about the orange flags, he told me, It is a sign for the Israelis to know that we are their allies. No whisky delivery for a while, hey, *Majnun?* He giggled.

Israeli jets flew over Beirut and bombed houses, hospitals, and schools. The radios trumpeted from every window on our street. On the West Side,

157

people were fleeing for their lives, and on our East Side, in the night, we could see flashes of resistance aiming at the skies. I went to the roof and looked at the west. The landscape was lit up under lightning bolts that fell from Israeli airplanes. There was one consistent line of red that reached to the sky. It never ceased, and I wondered if my uncle was shooting at the gods. And I wondered if cheap whisky bottles would turn into Molotov cocktails in Ali's hands.

I called Jallil Al-Tahouneh about my uncle's letter. He was brief on the phone, and rude. We decided to meet in front of Café Sassine. He said that he would pass with his car if I would wait for him outside. Then he asked me if I would be alone. I assured him that I would be.

Do not forget the envelope, he said.

I slammed the phone in his ear.

I waited outside the café. It was sunny, and I watched a group of girls existing the nuns' school in short skirts, holding books wrapped in thick elastic bands against their young breasts. They giggled in chorus, swung their fertile hips and their freshly shaved legs in a shared rhythm. Their wide brown eyes shifted and stole glances.

A car stopped in front of me, and a man with glasses and wearing a wool jacket leaned to the driver's side, opened the door, and called me by my last name. I got in. The man did not greet me.

He seemed nervous, or upset. I thought how he must be boiling with heat under the thick wool jacket. He was oblivious to my presence, but he stared at the envelope.

Is that it? he asked.

What? I asked back, knowing full well what he was looking for.

The envelope.

Yes.

He made a sudden turn and took the downhill road back to the Syriac neighbourhood.

He stopped the car, fixed his glasses, and snatched the envelope. Let me see.

He was boorish, and I felt annoyed by his eccentric ill manners.

He looked at me with his narrow eyes. Was this opened? he shouted.

No.

You opened it?

Yes.

Why? he shouted.

Because I felt like it.

You shouldn't have opened it.

All the money is there. Count it.

He started to count the money. Then he shoved the envelope in his pocket and said, Okay, leave now.

I pulled out my gun and replied, No, you leave.

He froze.

Listen, I am just doing this as a favour, I said. You haven't even said thank you. I am not walking all the way back on my feet, do you understand? I do not give a fuck about anything but respect. Respect is very important to me. I love respect, and I kill disrespect. You say one more word and I will shoot you and keep the money. Do you understand?

All of a sudden the man burst into a big smile. In a quick magic act of metamorphosis he turned from a cockroach into an apologetic hunchback, bowing his head, and calling me 'ustadh (teacher).

Your uncle is a dear friend, he said, a very dear friend, indeed. Here. He pulled out two hundred liras and smiled. This is for your trouble.

Drive back, I said, and make it fast.

Early one morning a few days and many more dead civilians on the West Side later, two militia-men knocked at my door.

Al-Amn A-Dakhili (internal security). Open up! they shouted from the other side. When I did, they stormed my house and pushed me against the wall. A man put a gun to my head. Two more searched the house.

What is it? I asked

Shut up, Hashash (drug user)! The man with the gun to my head slapped my face. You are coming with us. Abou-Nahra wants to see you.

Let me get dressed, I said.

The man with the gun pushed me.

I am coming! I said. Do you want me to meet the commander in my underwear?

He grabbed me by my shirt. Do it fast, he said.

I led him to my room, found my pants, and while he was shoving me, I slipped my finger inside the bundle of money in my pants pocket. I waited until he pushed me again, then pretended to fall and stashed the bundle under the old, heavy couch. Then he and the other men led me to the jeep. On the way down, Abou-Dolly, the grocer, was standing at the entrance shaking his head. *Zu'ran* (thugs), he said, and looked me in the eyes.

Why are you taking me? I asked my captors.

The man with the gun bounced around in his seat and grabbed my hair. One more word and I will make you spit blood from your mouth. Do you understand?

Eventually, we arrived at the *Majalis*. I got out of the jeep, and two militiamen led me down some stairs and underground. They shoved me into a room containing a table and couple of chairs. I sat on one of the chairs and waited.

Two hours passed, and still I waited. All I heard was the slam of a metal door, a few guard's steps, some moaning. I felt the dampness of the moist underground, the cold walls, the vague urine smells, and the unpainted concrete floors. I paced, and fidgeted, and changed chairs. Maybe they had found out about the poker deal. I should have killed Najib, that idiot; or had George stabbed me in the back again?

Soon I became vindictive. Was it the poker deals, or the envelope from my uncle to Jallil Al-Tahouneh?

I prepared myself for the coming slaps, the repetitive questioning. *Tell the same story, Bassam, tell the same story.* I craved a cigarette. Finally, I heard keys twisting inside the door lock, and Abou-Nahra came inside, smiling. He was accompanied by a guard.

Ah! You are Bassam. I thought it was you, he said from behind his glasses. I wondered if he could still see me by the room's dim lightbulb that almost touched his head under the low ceiling.

Stand up! his man shouted and slapped the back of my head. Stand up for the commander, *Hashash*.

I stood up slowly, looking Abou-Nahra straight in the eyes.

Kalb, stand up fast! The guard slapped me again on the head, pushed me, and kicked my shin. I lost my balance and fell to the floor. When I touched the grainy surface of the concrete I felt its coldness and dampness, and my clothes rubbed against it and picked up its grey colour, the soft grey grains that covered the rough, uneven surface. I wondered about the sloppy job they'd done of pouring concrete in that place. The floor was not even; maybe that is why all the chairs wobbled when I was sitting down, I thought, as feet landed on my face and battered my morning eyes.

I stood up, bleeding. Abou-Nahra waved his hand, and the monster stopped his *Dabkah* dancing on me.

Do you know what you did?

No.

Listen, I am a very busy man, and your uncle the *yassareh* (the leftist) was a friend of mine. You speak, or I will keep you here with Rambo.

I have no idea what I did.

Why did you kill the old man?

What old man?

His wife said there were things stolen.

Who? I have no idea what you are talking about.

Rambo came back and grabbed my hair, put his mouth in my ear and whispered, Talk now, or you will not be happy at all.

Okay, here is the story, little boy. Abou-Nahra leaned his glasses toward my face, and in a low, calm voice, he told me, Last night, Laurent Aoudeh was killed in his apartment. A burglary also took place. We interrogated his wife. She was at her friend's place in the mountains. Some African diamonds were stolen from the house.

Maybe she killed him! Maybe she stole them! I said.

Do not interrupt the commander! Rambo barked and hit me on the head.

When we pressed her, Abou-Nahra continued, she said that she suspected you. You pushed drugs on her. And you were hanging around with the old man lately. Do you like old, rich men?

No.

Yes, you do. Maybe you give him *massat* (blowjobs). People in the neighbourhood have seen you with him lately.

People like who? I asked in defiance.

The grocery man, Abou-Dolly, told us that you took a walk every day with him. We heard a great deal about you. Everyone knows that you are a *hashash*. Where were you last night?

Home. I did not do it.

We found a gun in your place. Listen, you little communist . . . You are a communist, aren't you, just like your uncle? You tell me where you hid the diamonds or Rambo here is going to show you the midday stars from inside the womb of your mother.

My mother is dead.

Rambo went berserk: Are you answering back to the commander, *ya kalb!* He beat me with the butt of his gun.

I fell on that cool floor again, and his boots came and retreated like waves that splash on misty shores, like black veils that eclipse the sun from your eyes, like the sound of blasting drums in your ears, like lollypop drips on your chin, like the smell of plastic erasers in your classroom. The dust from the floor rose again, like the powder chuck that was swept from the blackboard by that brown-nose Habib, oh, and like the slaps from the French Jesuit priest that landed on your palm as if they were the ruler's blessing, and like your bent knees on those narrow logs under the chapel benches, and like the smell of incense that came back and gave you a celestial high, and forgive me, Father, for I have sinned, I jerked that tree until it ejaculated fruits, I broke that glass with St Peter's rock, I stole candies, and I fumbled that little girl under the falling bombs in the shelter, while her mother was snoring in sync with the news on the radio. You see, Father, I confess, I am the one who waited until the candle was dead, and then I slipped my hand under her night-gown, to her newly acquired public hair, and she never said a word, and she followed me when I played, when I went up to the roof, she followed me like a puppy dog, like a female bird. Ever since then, Father, she dressed louder, played with her hair, chewed gum with an open mouth, danced flamboyantly to every jingle. She became jealous of my mother, of my young friends, and then, Father, suddenly one day she was repulsed by my husky voice, my puberty nose, my red pimples, and my swollen nipples. You see, Father, she grew up to hang out only with militiamen who came in stolen Italian cars, who honked under her father's window. And I, resentful of my age, of my poverty, resentful that she left me for older boys, would watch her rushing to their cars, to their golden rings, their dangling Christmas cedars that hung on their open chests, and their Drakkar Noir cologne, and their loud music tapes that offended the neighbourhood. Her hair, Father, flew from their topless cars, cars that drove them to their summer cottages on polluted beaches, and their mountain's *garçonnière*. And when she saw me, Father, she smiled at me like the little man in her dollhouse. So you see, Father, ever since I have refused to go down into the shelter, even if Rambo here hammers me into a meat pie. No, I won't go down to that dark place because I have always hated the underground and the little devils who dwell there, who made me lust for her skinny thighs and her newly acquired public hair.

Before Abou-Nahra left the room, he walked toward me and leaned over to the floor. I could barely see his face; everything was hazy. His glasses danced as if he were in a diabolic 1970s James Bond movie, and I heard his gangster voice: We will shake you and stir you . . . and all I need from you are the diamonds. Then we will let you go. Now, be a good comrade and share with Rambo your hiding place. I heard that communists like to share things, so here is your chance to be part of an egalitarian society. Do the right thing and make your communist uncle proud.

Abou-Nahra smiled, the door slammed, and I passed out.

When I came to, the brute guard led me to a small room that contained nothing but a blanket and a filthy toilet.

I could see from only one eye. I sat on the floor, swept the dust with my left hand, and let my right palm rest on the cool ground, channelling the temperature from my hand to my eye. My body ached; my lips bled.

I tried to sleep, but Rambo was determined to deprive me of sleep. He opened the door every few minutes to ask me to stand up.

If I see you sitting or sleeping I will stick your face in the toilet, he said. Do you understand, *Hashash*?

Walk! he shouted; and I walked back and forth.

For most of the night, the monster deprived me of sleep. I held the wall and tried to keep my body upright. When I fell on my knees, I tried to listen for the door latch. Before Rambo entered, I would pull my body up. When I fell asleep, he was furious and dragged me out of the cell to a bathroom. He filled the sink with water and pushed my head in it repeatedly. Once, when I was under water, I thought, Fuck him. When he pulls me back up I will not breathe. Fuck him, I thought, I will hold my breath and dive under the sea with the poisonous fish. I will stay there and watch the tourists passing in that cruise ship again. This time I will wear my best tuxedo and show those foreigners how I can swing, and wave my dancing stick in the air to those mambo tunes with a belly dancer on each side of my hips, with sexless angels who watch me with envy, with mocking nymphs, with whisky connoisseurs serving Saudis with trimmed goatees, with a few underground Playboy Bunnies with soft, white cotton tails. Fuck him. I will sleep in a cabin with two beds and room service. Fuck that brute. I just have to save a few bubbles from the effervescent water in the sink, and I will just swallow them for air, and wait underwater for the mambo tune to come back. That is what I will do.

But the monster would watch me, and slap me as I turned navy, the colour of the deep sea, the colour of my left eye, the colour of the uniform of the captain of the ship.

The diamonds, he kept on repeating. *Ya habbub* (beloved), why are you doing this to yourself? I cannot understand why people like to go through so much pain. Is it worth it? They are only stones . . . Listen, I hate to kill another Christian. We are all from the same bone here. Now, tell me where the diamonds are, and I will let you out, I will even send you back to your place in a taxi. Here, I brought you some soup. I will even let you sleep tonight, and I know in the morning you will wake up fresh, and tell me exactly where you hid them.

I did not steal them, I whispered through my broken teeth.

What did you say? I can't hear you, you are talking like a woman. Are you a woman who sucks old men's dicks! Then the monster grabbed my neck and glued his ear to my lips. Talk to me, *Chéri*, and we all can go home tonight.

I did not do it, I said.

Tomorrow, he replied, you will remember. I know you have forgotten now, because your head is not on straight, and you had too much to drink. Now sleep.

Although he left me after that, I could not sleep well. I kept on waking up. I was afraid that the monster might burst into my cell and ask me to walk again. In the morning, he showed up. He shoved me with his boots and said, Now, where are they?

I started to cry. I did not do it, I said. I do not know anything.

Okay, *Hashash*. I think you are the type of man who does not accept kindness. I was fair to you. Did you like the soup? Because that was your last food. Come with me. *Yallah!* He called his friend, and they dragged me to a civilian car.

You like BMWs, I heard. You would want to buy one when you sell the old man's stones, right? Here, we will take you for a drive.

They shoved me in the trunk and drove for a few metres. Then they stopped and a voice shouted, Rambo, where are you going?

We are going to finish the communist, Bassam something.

How are you going to finish him? the voice said, giggling.

Like Rambo, Rambo answered, and they all laughed out loud.

Then they drove fast and in circles, making loops. My head bumped into the spare tire, then I felt nauseous, and the smell of the clean leather made me even sicker. Dark, it was dark, dark like my parents' tomb. Fuck him, I thought, at least I will not be buried in the same place as they!

Then the car stopped. The monster turned off the engine and the trunk popped up by itself. I kept my hand over my eyes. The little light that pierced the trunk blinded me, and vertigo made me vomit.

The second man was furious: *Akhu al-sharmuta,* he dirtied the car! Look – he vomited all over.

I heard a gun being cranked, and the second man's voice said, I am going to finish off the garbage now.

But Rambo ordered him to wait. I am telling you, wait! Rambo shouted, and the two men scuffled with each other.

Go take a walk, *Ya Allah.* It is my car, and I will take care of it.

Rambo leaned his head inside the trunk and said in his usual sarcastic voice: Now, *Ya habbub,* do you remember where the stones are?

I did not answer; I vomited some more. The vomit felt like it was going inward, through my nostrils, splashing on my chest a mutant bowl of soup.

Okay, suit yourself, he said. You know, I could do you a favour by shooting you now. I know that is what you want, but I won't do it. You and me are not done yet. I have not introduced you to the electric charger yet. I promise you will glow like *Mariam Al-Adhra'* (the Virgin Mary).

And Rambo and his friend drove me back, and carried me to the cell.

★   ★   ★

Ten thousand slaps landed on my tender skin, and soup was vomited from my stomach like an infant's cereal from my mother's feeding arms, from her piercing eyes, from her demanding breath, from her contempt for my father the fatalist, the indifferent, the slow walker, the quiet man who burst through the door, late, in the dark, and landed slaps on my mother's feeding arms, her piercing eyes, her demanding breath, her contempt for my father the fatalist, the indifferent, the slow walker, the quiet man who burst through the door in the dark, like my torturer who landed slaps and offered me soup that was vomited from my stomach like an infant's cereal from my mother's feeding hands, from her demanding breath, from her contempt for my father the fatalist, the indifferent, the slow walker like his son in that cell, where he was forced to walk all night, asking for his mother's feeding arms, her piercing eyes, her demanding breath to save him from the breathless water, to pull him from the bathtub with the duck that floated between the bubbles, and the water slaps that shook the cruise ship, and splashed soap on its wooden deck where once upon a time two strolling Brits, from the rainy north, walked calmly in the moonless night toward the dining hall, before the served soup got cold, and before the jailer, who wore a white apron, burst into the kitchen and asked me to stand up, and not to sit on the job, and not to answer back, and not to steal from the passengers' purses, and not to fondle the teenage

171

girls, and the horny diamond wives, and to keep on chasing dust, sweeping the deck, cleaning tubs with effervescent gas that precipitated from my drowning face, from my wandering submerged lips that flapped like flying fish over the moonless sea.

Rambo opened the door and said, You are free to go, *Hashash*. He held the door open. You have two minutes to leave.

I stood up and walked slowly out of the room. Now, I thought, he will shoot me in the back and blame my corpse for trying to escape.

I walked down the hallway. A few other rooms stretched out on both sides. I had shared the same uneven floor, the same cold, moist walls with others who moaned underwater dolphin calls, who swam in the same sea with open eyes, watching the schools of purple bubbles floating by.

When I reached the end of the hallway, a man opened the gate for me. I struggled up the stairs, and through the blinding light I saw a silhouette of a woman. *Ah, my mother is here, I thought. The Rambo bastard must have insisted on a family gathering.* Then I heard Nabila's voice swearing at saints and savages. She met me halfway down the stairs and pulled me to her.

When Nabila took a close look at me, she became hysterical, which frightened me. Then she caressed my hair, and in the flood of light she cursed the militia, she cursed Abou-Nahra, she cursed Christ and his disciples. She managed to half-carry me to her car, and she drove me to her place. Once we got there, she laid me at the entrance. She went up, called Chafiq Al-Azrak, and they both carried me up the stairs.

CHAPTER 13

For a few days, Nabila washed me, fed me, and nursed me back to health.

You have to leave this place, she said. Get your passport. Do you have a place to go?

Go to my apartment and see if my money is still under the sofa, I said.

She came back with a bundle of cash in an elastic band. Where did you get this money from? she asked.

I saved it.

You know, looking at this money I might think it *was* you who killed that man, but I heard that in your absence someone shot his wife. A shepherd found her in the mountains with a bullet in her head. After that, I went to that brute Abou-Nahra and made a scene. Behind all his good manners, he is nothing but a thug.

Where is George? I asked.

He is away. He came by and told me that he was going north, camping. I have not heard anything from him.

What is going on at the other side?

Al-Gharbiyyah (West Beirut) is still under siege.

174

The Palestinians might surrender soon. And yes, I almost forgot: Nahla said two young guys were looking for you over at Julia's store.

Did she describe them?

No, not really. She just said they were young. She said one of them had a broken nose.

In the middle of the night, I woke up sweating and moaning.

The door opened, and Nabila entered with a flashlight in her hand.

It is me, Bassam. Nabila. You are having nightmares. Look at you sweating.

She gently stroked my face. Look what they did to you, those thugs. *Ya 'Um Al-Nur* (Mother of Light), look. And she touched my face, kissed my cheek, and put her arm around my shoulders.

I slipped my hand onto her thigh, and she let me. I searched for her lips. She kissed me, and breathed louder. I slipped my hand onto her breast, and she let me. I ran my hand over her breasts in haste, my lips like those of a hungry dog, and she breathed more heavily. Slowly, slowly, she whispered. Slowly, my little one, slowly on your bruises, do not hurt yourself, slowly, she repeated, motherly. I pulled at her nightgown, and drove my lips to her large, round nipples. She held my head and caressed my hair. I pulled her down, and she lay next to me while I grabbed her flesh with the urgency of a hungry puppy. She licked my wounds like a primitive healer. Her voluptuous

175

thighs opened, and I dove into her wetness; she held my head, and caressed my hair, and brought me to an infantile orgasm.

In the morning I heard Nabila shuffling pots and dishes in the kitchen. Her radio joined all the neighbours' radios in a single choir of bad news.

I stayed in bed, naked, hesitant, and embarrassed. Finally, I had to use the bathroom.

She heard the flush and asked me if I wanted coffee.

I mumbled something and went straight back to my room.

Nabila opened the door. In her bathrobe she came closer, sat on the edge of the bed, and said, Bassam, you have to go back to your place. Let me see your eye. You need a new bandage. Here, put on your clothes and start working on getting that passport . . . Go. There is nothing in this place. Go . . . Get a passport photo . . . Your money is in the drawer . . . Come eat before you leave. I washed your clothes.

Then she disappeared. She came back with a paper. She held my hand, opened my palm. She rolled the paper inside it, closed my fingers, and said, Keep this with you. If you ever reach France or Europe, go see this man. He is George's father. My sister never wanted anything to do with him. She was ashamed. She was stubborn and proud. She made a mistake in her youth. She never needed anyone . . .

Nabila shed a single tear, just one long, salty

drop, and before it reached the side of her lip, she scooped it stoically with her tongue. She looked me in the eyes and said, I want you to see him, for your sake and for George's sake. His name and number are here. If you do not find him at that number, still seek him out wherever he is. Promise me that. Promise me that you will.

I nodded. Without uttering a word, I promised.

In the afternoon, I walked down the stairs and into the street and went home. All my drawers had been emptied, a few vases broken, and my clothes dumped on the floor.

I called Joseph Chaiben. He told me to meet him that night, on a street corner outside of the neighbourhood.

I will pass by and pick you up, he said.

I waited, and Joseph passed and picked me up, as he said he would.

I sensed that he did not want to be seen with me, so I asked him about it.

Nothing personal, Bassam. But you know how it is with the *Majalis*. Once they have a red eye on you, all your friends are watched.

We drove outside the city and into the high mountains, where we parked and took a walk.

I need a gun, I said.

Listen, Bassam, it is not a good idea for you to get a gun right now.

Someone is on my case, I said. I need to have it soon. I can pay.

I will see what I can do.

We drove back into the city. When I climbed out of the car, Joseph called me back and said, Bassam, I won't ask too many questions, but I know you did not kill the old man.

Who did?

He did not answer me. Instead, he stepped on the gas and drove away.

For the next few nights, I went over to the building opposite mine and slept in the open air.

From the roof, I could see West Beirut on fire. The Israelis bombarded the inhabitants for days, orange light glowed in the night, machine-gun bullets left the ground and darted into the air in red arches. The city burned and drowned in sirens, loud blood, and death.

One morning Joseph sent me a sign; he wanted to meet.

We met, and he handed me a gun. I gave him money. Then I asked if he could help me in an operation. I confided that I was set on leaving Beirut, and I had an idea for a last hit to generate more money.

What kind of operation? asked Joseph.

Robbing the casino.

Majnun, he said. You are *Majnun*. I am not sure, Bassam. This is risky; we will be fucking with the *Majalis*.

Yes. But what have the *Majalis* done for you,

Joseph? I saw you on the barricades for weeks on end. You risked your life. And all these commanders are getting sports cars and chalets, filling their bank accounts. Look, you can hardly even buy food for your mother and your little sister and brothers. Think, Joseph. The war will be over one day, and they will be walking around in Armani suits, and what will we have? Do you think they will say, Oh yes, he was a good fighter for the Christian cause? Think about it. We can each get a good amount of cash.

Joseph remained silent.

Do you know the real name of a man named Rambo? I asked. He drives a black BMW, and he has a long scar on his face that goes from his eye down to his chin.

Yes, I know Rambo, he is an *ars*.

I need to find out where he lives.

Walid Skaff knows him well; Walid told me that he had been invited to a party once in Fakhra, up in the mountains, at Rambo's chalet. Rambo confiscated a chalet from some Muslim family that ran away.

Over the days, my wounds started to close, my muscles got stronger. Now I walked without pain, and my nostrils spat out the residue of water. The few bubbles that had stayed inside my mouth from the time when Rambo plunged my head like a submarine into the white porcelain of the yellow-stained tubs, those bubbles popped and

179

evaporated, and sounded like words. So I went back to my old job at the port. When I entered the grounds, the guard came over to me and said, Abou-Tariq wants to see you.

I walked over to Abou-Tariq's office and knocked at the door. He was facing a little brass stove, making coffee. He turned slowly, beckoned me in, and poured me a cup. I sat across from him at his desk.

Where have you been? he asked.

I was arrested.

He nodded. Yeah, I heard.

What happened?

Someone shot someone in the neighbourhood, and so they dragged me to the *Majalis*.

You know Abou-Nahra's men came and asked questions about you? They wanted to search your trunk. I said, No one searches anything here. When they entered, they walked as if they owned the place. No one fucks with me here, I said. I do not work for them. My orders come from the highest commander, Al-Rayess himself. I only take orders from Al-Rayess, I told them.

Abou-Tariq played with his large moustache, then continued in his northern dialect. I said to them, When you enter here, you leave your gun at the gate or I will not let you in next time. They did not like it. Listen, you are a hard worker, and if you really did what they accuse you of doing, you would not have returned to make a living here, right?

I nodded.

They beat you up badly, those punks, didn't they?

Yes.

There is an Italian boat coming tomorrow night. For a few days after that, we will be needing you. Be here. Tonight it is slow. Go home and rest.

The next evening, I went back to the port and worked. On my break, I went up to the deck and looked for the captain. Captain Ashraf, an Egyptian, was eating in the kitchen.

I sat down and said to him, I work here at the dock.

He looked at me. Yes?

I need to leave this place, soon.

Do you have a visa? he asked.

Where is your ship going? I asked in turn.

Marseilles. You have a visa to France?

No, I admitted.

I cannot let you come on board.

How can we work it out? I asked.

He kept his silence, ate some more. Eventually, he asked. They pay you well here?

I have money, I said.

Eight hundred, he said.

I have six hundred.

The captain did not answer. He stood up slowly to leave.

I can give you seven hundred, I said, and I would

be left with two hundred for when I got there, to face my destiny.

We leave on Sunday. *Twakkal ala Allah*, and bring a warm jacket. It gets cold on the deck at night.

CHAPTER 14

I was lying on my bed at home, in the middle of the night, when someone knocked at my door. It was my neighbour from next door. She was in tears. They killed him, she said. They killed Al-Rayess.

The highest commander of the Christian Lebanese forces had been assassinated on a visit to one of his political-party compounds. While he was inside meeting with his supporters, a bomb exploded and brought the whole building down. Meanwhile, in West Beirut, the Palestinians and the leftist forces had surrendered to the Israeli forces.

I listened on the radio to the burial of Al-Rayess, and the withdrawal of Palestinian forces from Lebanon to Tunisia. Women in East Beirut wore black, and they all wept.

Nabila phoned me to assure me that she had dreamed it all the night before. She was taking Valium because the news of the assassination made her sick and depressed. She told me that she had talked to George, and that George told her that they had caught a suspect. His name is

Al-Tahouneh, she said. Or something like that. A member of the communist Syrian party. They also found in his house architectural drawings of the foundation of the fallen building.

Joseph finally agreed to the money-making plan I had proposed to him. So I watched the casino for a couple of days. The militia money-collectors came every other evening – two of them, in a civilian car and wearing civilian clothes. When they went inside the poker place I crossed the street and took a look at their car to see if they carried weapons other than the ones stuck in their waistbands. When they came out, I followed their car from afar and memorized their route. They stopped at one other poker place, and then went straight to the *Majalis*. They took a long, unpaved side road that led to the headquarters.

The day after I traced the route, Joseph and I waited for Najib's poker-playing friend to come home.

Joseph went up to the roof of the apartment building; I waited across the street.

Soon we saw the guy park his car and go up the stairs. I whistled with my two fingers in my mouth, and Joseph came down the stairs from the roof, coughing, and with a handkerchief on his face. When he passed Najib's friend, Joseph pretended to cough and then hit him in the face.

I flew up the stairs with thick tape in my hand.

Before Najib's accomplice could make a sound, Joseph stuffed his handkerchief in his mouth. I tied his hands and ankles, and we dumped him up on the roof of his building. I took his car keys. We got in the car and drove fast toward Joseph's place. Joseph went up to his apartment and brought down his *kalash* and guns.

As I drove, Joseph filled the gun magazines with bullets. He checked my gun and his. We stopped at the poker place and watched the two collectors go in. Then we drove ahead, onto the unpaved road that led to the *Majalis*.

I opened the hood of the car and blocked the street. I stood behind the open hood, and when I saw the collectors' car coming, I pulled a stocking over my head. Joseph hid in the ditch.

The collectors stopped their car and came toward our car, cursing. Joseph ran up behind them with his Kalashnikov.

Ala alaard ya ikhwat al-sharmuta (on the floor, you brothers of bitches), I shouted as I appeared from behind the hood with two guns in my hands, pointed at their faces. *Ala alaard*, I repeated.

Ala alaard, before I empty my guns on you, Joseph echoed from behind me.

The men lifted their arms in the air and then went down on their bellies. I put my foot on the first one's neck and pulled out his gun while Joseph frisked the other.

We tied their hands with tape and left them beside the car with the open hood. Then I drove their car, with the money inside, in reverse. I swung it around and drove it back the way it had come, stopping at an empty factory on the way. We left the car at the factory after pulling out the moneybags. We emptied everything in a delivery van that we had parked there during the day and drove the van away into the mountains.

Finally, we stopped. I counted the money and split it in half on the spot.

There is a ship leaving for France tomorrow. I am taking it, I told Joseph. Here, you go see Nabila. You know Nabila, right? De Niro's aunt?

Yes.

Give her my house keys. Tell her to take care of the house. Tell her I will look for the person whose name she gave me. I will keep my promise; tell her that. Now, leave me at the intersection down the hill. I will take a cab; it is better that we go our own ways.

Joseph and I kissed, and we separated.

Majnun, I will never forget you. *Majnun!* he shouted and drove away.

I took a taxi up the mountain to Fakhra. I stopped in the centre of the village, filled a can with water from the little stream that sang at night under the villagers' huts, and slipped into the bush and yet farther up the hills. Finally I stopped, poured water on the earth, made a pool of mud and smeared my face and hands with it. I walked all night through the houses in the village looking for a black BMW with tinted glass. I slipped behind the houses when the dogs barked. Then I passed through the dark alleys between the chalets. I covered the whole village, but I couldn't find the car. Early in the morning, I sat on top of the hill and watched the passing cars.

I saw a BMW speeding up the hill. It was driven as if by a drunk, in zigzags, like a donkey climbing uphill.

I ran after the BMW, through the pine trees, through the moist hills, through the morning dew, pushing away the loose branches. I crossed the stone stairs and waited until the car stopped. A man opened the door and slowly stepped out of it. It was Rambo.

I walked toward him, and when he heard my steps he looked back and pulled out his gun in slow motion. I stopped. I saw his face, and my heart started to beat with sounds of death and drums. I felt as if I should walk all night again, and crush every mattress that would call me to sleep, and the sweat fell from my forehead and soaked my face in a bucket of cool liquid, and the morning breeze swept past me with jasmine scent. Rushing butterflies flapped their gigantic wings, raising the mountain's fog from the valleys, and my eyelids fluttered. My hands stretched forward, both of my index fingers squeezed the trigger, and I shot at him. He smiled as I emptied my magazine, and the bullets flew and plunged into his cologne-scented flesh, his whisky's final sighs, and his nails that gripped the door handle of his car.

My gunshots rang through the deep valley with the sound of mourning bells, with the crack of hunters' rifles in the morning sun. I shot him until he fell to the ground, and the thickening fog passed us by and carried his last breath.

I searched Rambo for his car keys and found them under his body. I touched his leat her jacket, his white silk shirt, now turned brown with a mix of blood and red earth. His eyes watched me for the last time. I saw my image sinking down into his black pupils, and it frightened me.

I picked up the keys and drove his car down the slopes. Then I pulled over to the edge of the road, stepped out of the car, and vomited over the edge of a cliff. My head was pulled down to the earth, and I was on my knees.

The ship was leaving that night. After I returned home, I packed a few of my clothes, picked up my passport and money, and went down the stairs for the last time. The neighbour women were splashing water up and down the marble. The water had come on that day, and there was water on the roofs and coming down the faucets, and the neighbour women had taken their buckets to the roof and carried them down full. Some looked at me, and some did not. I knew what was in their minds; I knew whose two hands and whose bucket were missing. I tiptoed over the little stream of water and soap. I rushed, and I didn't say a word to the women. I did not greet, I did not thank,

I did not scrub, I did not carry. I stepped over the water, seeking the seas.

I walked down the street. Nothing changes here, I thought. Those windows will last forever. Cars will multiply, park, and grow like plants, like colourful sidewalk trees. I did not look around me, I did not greet anyone or cry. I was just leaving.

A car passed by me, and then it stopped and came back. It was De Niro. He asked me to hop in.

I told him that I was fine, that I had to go to work.

I will drive you. We need to talk, he insisted. His eyes were red. He was either drunk or high, or maybe he couldn't sleep from the noise of gunshots, the stomping drum of military boots.

When I asked him to leave me alone, he got out of the car, held me, and kissed my forehead. He told me, You are my brother. He walked me to the other side of the car, sat me in the passenger seat, then walked back to the driver's side, touching the car on the way with one of his palms – a palm that had been laid on my neck, on my cheek, the same palm that had guided me to his car.

He drove fast. He did not stop, he did not brake. He looked at me, at times smiling, at times almost crying. He stayed silent until we passed Quarantina, and then he swung the car down to the highway that ended under the bridge, and he drove fast again, shifting gears and jerking the car.

He slowed down, and we drove under the bridge, and he parked the car just behind its large concrete foundation. The sewer that carried our collective sins ran beside us.

We both remained silent, facing a large pile of sand and rocks and unfinished construction. George's handgun lay beside us on the seat.

Then George started to laugh. He still could not look me in the eyes. He pulled out two cigarettes, lit them both, and handed me my share.

There was fresh blood on his military pants; a large black patch of it almost glowed.

He saw me looking at it. He reached for a bottle of whisky and drank some. When he offered it to me, I declined.

I killed today, he finally said.

I nodded without surprise.

I killed many. Many, he said as he played with his gun.

I nodded again and kept my silence for a moment longer. Then: I have to go, I said. I was no longer interested in hearing the sounds of the slaughterhouses, the rush of thick heels, the fireworks. I could only hear waves splashing over the bridge, bouncing on the car windshield, moving toward my feet.

George pulled out a tube, and using a little spoon that fished powder, he sniffed. He passed the back of his palm over his nose, then looked at the nose in the mirror. Turning, he smiled at me and said, Ten thousand. Ten thousand, maybe more, he mumbled. We must have killed ten thousand of them.

Who? I asked.

Children, women, we even shot the donkey, he said and laughed.

What happened, George? I asked, giving in.

He grabbed the gun and aimed it at the windshield, then looked at it and released a muffled laugh.

Talk, I said. If that is why you brought us here.

I will tell it all, he said. I will tell it all . . . We attacked a Palestinian camp and killed by the hundreds, maybe thousands.

When?

These last few days.

How? Why? I asked.

We camped at the international airport in Lebanon. International, he repeated and laughed again. All week, after the assassination of Al-Rayess, we didn't sleep. The men screamed for revenge. An Israeli liaison officer, Eitan, came by with Abou-Nahra. He said that there were still a few armed pockets in the Palestinian camps after the surrender. Abou-Nahra said, We have to purify the camps.

George laughed, and held the gun, and spun its barrel. De Niro's a fucking good actor; you remember that scene in that movie, Bassam, when De Niro played his best friend? You are my best friend and my brother, you are.

He tried to hug me, but I pushed him away.

He continued. Fifteen hundred lions positioned at the airport we were. Nothing would stop us, nothing. We moved like thunder toward the Sabra and Shatilla refugee camps, along the wide road through Ouzai. We passed the Henri Chehab military compound, and another unit met us from the south army, men from the villages of Damour, Saadiyat, and Nameh. Those men never forgot their burned villages, those men were also lions. One of them, an older fellow, looked me in the eyes and said, We have been waiting a long time for this. So we killed! We killed! People were shot at random, entire families killed at dinner tables. Cadavers in their night-clothes, throats slit, axes used, hands separated from bodies, women cut in half. The Israelis surrounded the camps. And then an Israeli lieutenant named Roly, who was stationed near Bir Hassan, across from the stadium, sent a message to the camp committee to have all our men bring their weapons to the stadium. We told him that we do not take orders from him. We told him that orders came from Abou-Nahra, and that the high Israeli command knew about it. We moved farther in, and Israeli aircraft dropped eighty-one-millimetre illumination flares. The whole area was lit up; it was like being in a Hollywood movie. And I am De Niro in a movie, George said. Drink, he suddenly shouted at me. Drink!

I waved the bottle away from my face.

He drank, then spoke again. Everything was

fluorescent white; you could see like it was daylight. The sky was glowing as if the Messiah himself had showed up. The units from the south were already inside. At the Akka hospital, some of our men followed the wounded to finish them off. When we arrived, we heard the scream of a woman. Three guys were raping a nurse on a doctor's table. An Asian doctor had a photo of Arafat in his office; he started to speak in English to me. I said, Terrorist! You are a terrorist, and you have a terrorist photo on the wall. He spoke to me in English again. I beat him up with the handle of my gun.

De Niro drank some more. Outside, he said, bodies rolled in sand, bloated. Blood turned into dark stains, green flies were feeding, bulldozers dug and shoved cadavers in ground holes. It was all like a movie. All like a movie. Dead people everywhere. Do you still want to hear? Do you want to hear more? More? He shouted at me, Here, drink! He cranked his gun and put it in my face. Drink, I say.

I took the bottle and sipped.

What is my father's name? he asked me.

I do not know.

Yes, you do. You are a liar. You talk to Nabila, you visit her when I am not there. I saw you. Do you want to hear more? Here, drink more. Yes, you want to hear, and I want to finish my story. We tied men together with a rope and shot them in the head one by one. Dogs snatched cadaver parts and escaped behind little alleys. A fucking Syrian pushed past with his cart, selling vegetables. I asked him his nationality. It was Syrian! Fucking Syrians! They all come here to take our land! I kicked his vegetable cart. Abou-Haddid did not even waste time; he put a bullet in the Syrian's stomach. Everyone against the wall, I said. Women started to scream, begging us, telling us that they had already surrendered. Kamil grabbed one of them by the hair, pushed her on the floor, and stepped on her neck. I don't want to hear a sound here, I shouted to them.

Everyone to the stadium. On the way, some of those fighters laughed and tossed hand grenades into the middle of the crowd.

After telling me this, George brooded for a while. He was becoming even more intoxicated. He talked, and then he stared into emptiness. He drank more, and then he mumbled. He mumbled something about his mother, that he had killed her. He began to hallucinate, and looked sad all of a sudden. I thought he was getting tired, so I tried to pull the gun away from his hand, but the moment I touched it, he bounced up and threatened to shoot me. I thought he would.

I killed my mother, I killed her, he said and burst into tears.

Your mother died in the hospital from cancer, I said to him.

For Al-Rayess! he shouted, lifting the bottle and drinking some more.

I have to go, I said.

No one is going anywhere, not before I finish talking, he said. Listen to what happened there in that camp. Listen. Kamil had cocaine. We sniffed, and we shouted, For Al-Rayess! We rounded up more men against a wall, women and children against another wall. We shot all the men first. The women and children wailed, and we changed magazines and shot them as well. It was their cries that made me shoot them. I hate kids' cries. I never cry; have you ever seen me cry? The rest who came after, when they saw the corpses on the floor, they panicked. Some pissed in their pants. I saw three fleeing from the back; we chased them in the narrow alleys. I became separated from the others, and I lost everyone; I was alone. I broke down doors. I entered a house and found a woman on the floor surrounded by her dead daughters. She looked me in the face. I said, You want to join your family, don't you? She said, You might as well finish what you started, my son.

My son! My son, George said and laughed. I hit her with the butt of my rifle, many times, many times, like this (and he punched the air with his gun). Blood sprang from her head like a hose; it splashed on my thighs. I wandered through the alleys alone. I saw a woman putting her hand over her children's mouths . . . They cried. The houses were filled with bodies of slain women in aprons, men stretched next to their wives and their raped daughters. Then I stopped. You wouldn't believe it, but I heard the cooing of a partridge bird, just like the one we hunted up in the mountains, you and I, Bassam, you and I. I followed it through the narrow walls. It ran, and I ran after it; it hopped above cadavers soaked in streams of cooking water. I saw it flying over the olive trees, above the hills. And then it stopped, and came back, and perched on top of a dead man's body. I saw the hand of a dead man reaching up to caress its feathers.

I saw it! George shouted and took another sip. I chased it again, and it entered a hut. I ran inside, and I saw it slip under a bed. I lifted the mattress; two small children were huddled in fear under there. Their dead mother's body was in the room, staring at them with open eyes. I just wanted to hunt the bird, George said. All I wanted was to hunt.

Then he was silent, brooding. He pulled out his magnum, opened its barrel, took out two bullets, spun the barrel, and said to me, Three out of five. Game now, here.

I declined. I tried to pull the gun from his hand, and he called me a coward.

You are not a man, George said, and that is why your woman was looking for someone who is a man. He pointed the gun at my head. Coward! he taunted me.

The only coward here is you, I said.

He looked me in the eye. Then he said, You are leaving. I see your bag. You think you have to go. Your face is all cut. Your eye has a scar.

196

It is from your boss, I said. It is his goodbye gift to me. You have killed. I know you have killed. You killed that old man as well. And his wife. You always killed.

We always killed, Bassam, George replied. He looked me in the eyes again and repeated, *We* always killed. The man who killed Al-Rayess, that man confessed. He mentioned your name. You gave him the plan for the foundation. *You* killed Al-Rayess.

That is why you came? I asked him.

Yes, I came to take you to the *Majalis*. They want you back there. You know, a few more bubbles. A few more slaps.

So, why did you drive in this direction? I asked him. The torture chambers are on the other side.

No, Bassam, the torture chambers are inside us. But I am fair, and you are my brother. I will give you a way out, De Niro said. I took Rana from you, he said, and he pointed his gun, and his eyes emitted red like blood, harsh as a stone, veiling lives, and shining in the windshield's light.

PART III

PARIS

CHAPTER 15

I arrived at the port and went to find the ship. I looked for the Egyptian captain.

There you are, he said. Do you have the money?

I paid him, and he led me down to the engine room. This is Moustafa, the mechanic. You stay here with him until the ship leaves the port, then you go up on the deck. We are leaving soon, the captain said. He climbed back upstairs.

Then the engine roared and chuckled, and the pipes swelled and ticked, and Moustafa smiled at me and said, First time on a ship?

Yes.

He laughed. If you feel dizzy, go up and get some fresh air. He smiled again.

The boat moved slowly into the sea.

A couple of hours passed, and during all that time I sat very still and made my mind blank. I wanted it to stay blank for a long time.

Finally, I went up on the deck and watched the little light on the shore fading into the black of the night. A few sailors rushed up and down the stairs and onto the decks. I watched them and held my bag, my money, my gun, and my jacket on my knees.

The air was still, and the ship sailed quietly from darkness and into darkness, from water into water, from earth into earth. I watched the slow death of the distant twinkles on the land.

Ten thousand waves passed under the floating tank that moved away from my home.

Ten thousand fish sang underneath the waves and nibbled on the garbage thrown from the cook's hand.

I looked at the sky. It was covered with light signals from faraway planets bursting with gas and the happy bonfires of dead humans singing warriors' songs in a landscape of burning rocks, and sending Morse code signals to ships steered by alcoholic captains into islands inhabited by sirens who sing in cabarets and offer up their salty sex organs that taste like the marinated fish of Sunday's family gatherings after the families have endured the moralistic discourse of fat priests who douse congregations with incense spilled from the pendulum motion of their jerking hands, a motion that rocks like the swings in parks that are swamped with baby strollers pushed by Filipino nannies on temporary visas and with small paycheques that are transferred at Christmas to faraway families who live in huts by the sea and receive Morse code signals from those old creatures from astral space. The creatures read oracles and long letters home from nannies who watch the kids of executives pouring sand in plastic buckets and climbing geometrical cubes in red-striped sailor's shorts, and the creatures can also explain letters home from orderlies dressed in white aprons who cruise the elevators in old folks' homes, changing the sheets of senile, retired sea captains and society ladies, who are in complete ignorance of the presence of their three-piece-suited sons and oblivious to the repetitive, high-pitch complaints of their daughters-in-law, complaints like those of seagulls that feed on the sea trails of sailors' food, and rest on the deck, ogling me with xenophobic eyes, sharpening their beaks, and taking off to other planets on mythological wings.

Moustafa sought me out, sat next to me, and offered me a cigarette.

I have seen passengers vomiting for days; you do not get seasick. You are leaving. He smiled.

Yes, there is nothing for me there.

Yes, there is nothing in these places, he agreed.

We smoked, and Moustafa walked down to the stern of the ship, above the ceaseless waves that passed under our fleeing feet.

The little lamps went off, and only the captain's room shone in the middle of the sea. The wind got cooler, so I went downstairs, through the narrow alleys, and sat in the kitchen. The captain came down slowly and sat, pensive and calm. Then he stood up, filled a kettle with water, and offered me tea.

I have a cabin for you, he said. You can have it after eleven. Mamadou, the African sailor, has a shift at eleven, and you can lie down in his bed.

We drank tea in silence. At eleven, I followed the captain. He banged on a cabin door, and an African man slowly opened up. The captain explained the situation to him. Mamadou nodded and waved his hand to invite me in. I lay on the bed and tried to sleep through the sound of the omnipresent engine, a sound that was loud but muffled like underwater signals from a clanking factory buried under seven layers of seas. I imagined a factory with armies of slave monkeys packing tuna in metal cans, and sticking on labels with esoteric languages, and arranging the cans in waterproof musical boxes screeching diabolic symphonies, and shipping them on the backs of seahorses to underwater villages filled with drowned soldiers, kidnapped maids, invading barbarians, treasure hunters, and a princess who had been enslaved in a sealed bottle by a jinni with a single earring, and who was now waiting for a fisherman to solve the riddle and take her back to her lost palace, where she would rejoin the caliphate in a garden of jasmine and amber, and stroll through the arches of Baghdad before the invading armies burned her favourite books and destroyed thousands of tales.

★　★　★

In the morning, Mamadou knocked at the cabin door, and we exchanged places. As I was stepping out, he smiled and said that the last passenger had refused to share his bed with a black man. He shook his head and smiled again.

I went up to the deck. The ship was surrounded by blue water and blue sky, and nothing else. Sailors rushed along the deck, and up and down the metal stairs. The boat cut its way through water that merged with the sky.

Moustafa found me on the deck and asked if I had eaten. No, I said.

We went down to the kitchen, and the cook offered us food in plastic bowls. The boat rocked, and the dishes swung in our hands, and the food shifted side to side in our mouths. Everyone was silent. The engine's hum cut through the sailors' bashful eyes, their quiet manners and balanced feet. After a time, a blue-eyed sailor spoke to Moustafa in broken English, saying something about the boiler in the back. Moustafa stood up and slowly shuffled his feet. The man sat in Moustafa's place and started to eat, ignoring my presence. I finished my food and walked up to the deck. The wind had risen. The smell of water surrounded the boat. I sat and thought of my home. I tried to locate its direction but found I was lost in the roam of the drifting-away earth, as if my neighbourhood drifted on the tide, and my chunk of land, with its war and my dead parents, floated on the seas. I stretched my neck, and stood on my toes, but could not see it; it floated away all around me, it was swept away in the flux of things. I leaned over the rail and watched white foam passing the bottom of the ship, caressing its edges and changing shape. And a partridge appeared and said to me, *No condition is permanent. I shall bring you a branch when the floating mountains are closer to your feet.*

I paced the deck, the splashing waves staining my face in ocean blue, and when the boat rose above a high wave I stretched out my hand, and touched the sky, and pulled it down, and took a peek over it, and released it. It bounced back, fluttered, and settled again.

When night returned, Moustafa sat next to me and asked, Do you like a little *kayf* (hash)?

I nodded and smiled.

He pulled out a small bag, and we rolled oily hash into a thin sheet that we cut, with giant scissors, from the drape of the stretched-out sky. Moustafa passed his tongue along the edge of the sheet, and the liquid, like carpenter's glue, sealed it. I extended my arm and picked a light from a burning star, and Moustafa grabbed the wind and squeezed it in his chest. Then he passed the wind, the sky, and the fire to me, and I pulled all these toward my lips, and like a black hole I sucked them in, held them, released them. They floated and landed on the water's surface, bounced on the waves, and attracted a school of flying fish that circled inside the fumes and sang ultraviolet, watery melodies to the enslaved underwater monkeys who repeated the tunes over the pounding noises of the tuna machines, sweet tunes reminiscent of the jungle sounds in their long-destroyed habitats, their abodes in swaying branches.

You will never go back. You seem like the wandering type to me, my brother, Moustafa said to me.

What is there to go back for? I whispered.

I have been on the seas for many years, Moustafa told me. I left Egypt when I was young. I have travelled places, my friend. I went to Japan and saw glittering lights, I had massages with tiny women walking on my back, I went to Africa and got drunk in bordellos, I slept with whores of all colours in all continents. I wasted my money on restaurants and bars, I smoked opium and snorted the best cocaine. I worked on many ships. I have seen prostitutes with black eyes like deep wells who asked me to save them from the fists of their gold-toothed pimps. I have walked in cities where men's arms were stamped with anchor tattoos, and women perched on windowsills, calling out to you to make haste before their husbands returned.

Moustafa and I smoked and told stories, and for days the ship slid over the waves, and waves passed by and never came back, and the sailors pulled their sails, and the wind puffed and huffed and pushed us north and stole the smoke from our breath, and when the winds were high up, the sea slowed down and the water slowed, and the sail slowed, and the fish slowed, and the partridge glided above our heads under the sheet of the Hellenic skies, and one-eyed nymphs saw us and gathered to listen to our fantastic tales, charmed by the smell of our burning plants, mistaking it for the incense of their flying gods.

Two days before our arrival in Marseilles, the partridge took flight and disappeared.

CHAPTER 16

When the boat arrived in port, a group of the sailors led me down to the engine room. I stayed behind the boiler, sweating, and hid from the inspector who checked the cabins. When the inspector left, Moustafa and Mamadou ran to me and brought me water, laughing at my wet hair and clothes.

That night, Moustafa and I sailed to shore in a small boat. We crossed a fence and some train tracks. Then Moustafa smiled and said, You are in Marseilles. You are on your own now.

I walked.

I walked through vacant streets, past doors that opened directly onto the curb of the street. A few dogs barked at my passage. My shadow was pasted to the ground; it moved and shifted shape depending on the position of the street lamps that hung high on curved poles. A car passed me by; loud music blasted my ear and then faded behind the buildings when the vehicle made a sharp turn. I walked on, looking for the centre of the city, for a place where I could rest. I looked at the sky:

the purple light of dawn was starting to break, rising from underneath the sea. Then I heard that same bombastic music approaching again. I recognized the sound of the car without looking behind me. I grabbed my bag, switched it from my back to my belly, opened its useless lock, dug both of my hands into it, and cranked the gun inside the bag.

I could tell, from the stretch of the headlights on cobblestones, from the slow passing twilight on the doors of houses, that the car was slowing down behind me. I kept on walking. The car drove up beside me. Three kids were in it, and they all stared at me. The driver's hand was extended from the window like the hands of our taxi drivers from car windows back home. The two passengers shifted their heads to get a better look at me.

I heard one of them saying, *Une merde de beur ici chez nous.*

Hey, the driver called in French, we do not want filth like you here.

I looked him in the eye, said nothing, and kept on walking.

The kids cursed at me and drove away fast. At the top of the street, the car made a U-turn. Its lights beamed in my face. The kids opened their doors, got out of the vehicle, and slowly walked toward me. Their long, evil shadows touched the tip of my shoes; they swung sticks and pipes in their arms.

I turned and ran in the opposite direction, away

from the car lights that were blinding me. I heard rushing steps on the ground behind me, and promises to bash my head and stomp my body with heels.

When I turned the corner, I stopped in the middle of the narrow street, between two houses. I could hear dogs barking on the horizon. I waited for my pursuers. They rounded the corner and stopped suddenly when they saw me. I kept my gun hanging behind my back, and when they approached me, tapping their sticks on their palms, flashing their sarcastic smiles, telling one another jokes, and mocking my masochistic tendencies, I pulled it out slowly. I cursed my pursuers in my own language, and waved my hand, daring them to accept that my bullets would kiss their high boots, shred their leather jackets, enlighten their shaved heads, rewrite their tattoos, colonize their souls, twist their skin like water faucets, block holes like Tuma's fingers, and make them sing a church-choir tune.

The one farthest from me ran off, and I was left with two of them walking backwards in fear, their pipes and their sticks bent toward the ground like thirsty flowers.

I smiled and waved my gun in their pale faces. I cursed their mothers and their great-grandfathers, and ordered them to drop their pipes and their sticks. I made them kneel on the ground, and when they did that, I asked them to take off their shoes and their pants.

Les pantalons aussi, sharmuta, I shouted, and dogs barked behind doors. A few lights appeared in kitchens and above doorsteps, and curious faces filled small, square windows. Women in see-through nightgowns parted theatrical curtains and peeked out their heads with a playwright's nervousness.

I kicked both the kids, and then I walked away fast with their shoes in my hand. When I reached the street where I had been walking, I threw away the shoes, and I ran through foreign alleys and avenues. I ran until dawn, until finally I settled on a bench on the promenade, and listened to the sea, and watched the slowly changing colours of the sky.

By mid-morning, the sun shone strong, which made the city shadows darker. I saw Manichaean split walls, sparkling tree leaves, and shaded benches. The cafés opened, and people strolled onthe promenade. I walked beside them, passed them, and then slowed to walk again with them. I looked for a place to exchange money, and found one. I did my exchange and walked to a café. There, I sat and I ate and I drank and I looked at the newspaper. The old owner behind the bar did not seem surprised to see me. I walked on again and decided to look for a place to stay.

I entered the first hostel I saw, and the woman behind the desk, a large woman who looked in-different, or bored, asked me for identification.

I said that I would get it from the car. I stepped outside and never went back.

Instead, I wandered the whole day, aimless. I looked at people and shifted from one café to another. Finally, I searched my pocket for a light and pulled out the paper that Nabila had given me. On it, there was a name: Claude Mani. There was also a number, and on the bottom of the paper: Paris.

Suddenly it hit me – how far I was from Nabila, that I had left Beirut. At the same time, this realization gave me a sense of purpose. I decided to call the number, like I had promised. I found a telephone booth and dialed. The phone rang, but no one answered. Still I stood in the booth, looking with an empty gaze through the glass. I felt as if I could live inside of the booth, feeling its borders, claiming it for myself. I pretended that I was talking on the phone, but all I wanted was to be in the booth. I wanted to stand there and watch every passerby, I wanted to justify my existence, and legitimize my foreign feet, and watch the people who passed and never bothered to look or wave. I did not recognize a soul. So I waited and glued the receiver to my ear and listened to the long, monotonous tone. I listened until the recording of a lady's voice came on and gave me two choices: dial again or hang up.

I chose the former, and this time, a soft woman's voice answered.

I am looking for Monsieur Mani, I said in French.

The woman paused, then said, Monsieur Mani is dead.

We were both silent.

Who is calling? she continued after a moment.

I am a friend of his son, George, I said carefully.

There was another pause, and then the woman asked, Where are you calling from?

Marseilles.

I am Monsieur Mani's wife, she said.

I have a message for Monsieur Mani, I said. I didn't know what else to say.

Are you from Lebanon?

Yes.

There was a final pause. Then: Can you come to Paris? My daughter and I would like to meet you.

I took the bus to Paris. It passed through fields of vines that were arranged in rows. The vines curled around batons dangling white, and sometimes red, grapes through green leaves. We passed rustic villages with brick roofs, and churches perched on modest dunes, and clean, open spaces that seemed to have no purpose but to provide scenery for the occasional balancing villager pedalling a bicycle with a basket filled with vegetables. The bus stopped at a few small villages, and passengers entered and left quietly, aloof, like tourists on church visits. I sat alone, and leaned my head against the window, and slept. When I arrived in Paris, I got off the bus and looked for the woman I had talked to on the phone.

She wore a long navy dress, as she had promised. I approached her, and she smiled.

Do you have any luggage? she asked.

No.

The car is on the other side. She walked beside me, smiling. I am Genevieve, she said. Claude's wife.

I nodded.

When did you arrive in France?

A few days ago.

You came straight from Beirut?

Yes.

Yes, I knew the city a long time ago, before the war. I knew Beirut; it was a beautiful place.

In the car, I examined Genevieve. She was in her late forties, maybe her early fifties; she was well dressed and well made up, which made it hard to tell her age exactly.

She looked in the mirror constantly, and then before she took a turn she looked back at the rear window, then quickly glanced at me.

So you know George?

Yes, we were good friends.

He asked you to get in contact with Claude?

No, it is his aunt Nabila who gave me the number.

And George's mother?

She is dead.

Genevieve nodded slightly.

When we arrived at our destination, she parked the car and asked me to follow her. She opened the gate of a large, old, white building, and we walked through the entrance to the elevator. It was small and made of red wood and massive steel. Through the metal grid I could see a large spiral stairwell behind the ascending cage, and when the box arrived on Genevieve's floor (after being pulled up by demons who lived on the roof, I supposed), it gave an echoing screech like the kind one only expects to hear in large hallways suitable for chamber music, or in aristocratic ballrooms. Genevieve placed a key in the lock of her door, but before she got the chance to twist it, the door opened from the inside. A maid greeted the madame.

Genevieve invited me in and asked me to sit down.

I sat, and she disappeared. The maid brought me juice and some biscuits.

I drank, and ate, and looked at the high ceiling, the oriental carpets, the large Japanese paintings, the mahogany and cherry woods. I stood up and slowly made my way to the window, and from there I gazed down at the street. It stretched away on both sides, lined with balconies and small cars, and the white traffic lines that make Paris look symmetrical and divided.

Do you like the view? Genevieve asked me as she came back into the room.

Yes.

Where are you staying here? Do you know someone in town?

No.

Did you come by plane?

No, by boat.

Oh, mon Dieu, c'est long ça, non? she said in her pleasant, gentle voice. I noted her graceful manners, and her long robe, and her well-brushed, chestnut hair.

I promised Nabila that I would come and meet her brother-in-law, George's father.

Nabila is George's aunt? she interrupted.

Yes.

Listen, she said. Like I told you, George's father is dead, but my daughter, who is George's half-sister, is coming here, and she is dying to meet you. She is on her way. Maybe you can tell us everything when she comes? We will have dinner together. Do you want to take a shower? I can give you some clothes.

The bathroom had golden faucets; the water ran in abundance. I spread the foam of perfumed soap on my skin, and silky soft shampoo on my curly hair. The maid knocked, giggled, and handed me a razor. As I shaved, I let the water run in a vengeful act of waste. Then the maid knocked again and handed me pants, a shirt, and socks. The sleeves of the shirt were a little big and covered the back of my hands; I folded them up, put on the socks, and walked out.

I heard two women's voices conversing in the living room. I entered, and they both stopped and smiled at me. A young woman stood up, approached me, and kissed me on the cheeks. She had long fair hair and George's eyes.

I am Rhea, she smiled. George's sister.

I recognized you, I said.

Really? Do I look like George?

Your eyes, I said.

She smiled, and held my arm, and said, Let us eat.

We sat, and Genevieve poured wine to fill our glasses. We are in silence for a while, and then Rhea spoke. Her words cut through the clang of heavy silver spoons that dived to the bottom of gold-rimmed plates and the sound of wine pouring into towering crystal glasses.

My mother told me that you came by boat, she said.

I nodded.

Why did you leave? she asked.

The war, I said.

And is George happy there?

He never wanted to leave.

My father tried to bring him here, you know, but George's mother resisted, and when the war broke out we never knew what happened to them. My father tried to send messages through the embassy, but it seemed as if George's mother never wanted to have anything to do with us.

I kept quiet.

Monsieur Bassam is a man of small words, Genevieve teased me.

Ask and I will answer, I said.

Ah, bon! she shouted and laughed.

So what does George do? asked Rhea.

He does security.

Quoi? Mother and daughter looked at each other in surprise.

Do you mean he is a bodyguard?

Sort of.

C'est dangeneux, ça, non? Genevieve murmured from inside her tilted, suspended, swinging wine-glass. A burgundy wave waited on the coast of her lips for the word to leave.

Do you have a photo of him?

No.

Is he tall?

A bit taller than me.

So, were you two together in the security business?

No, we were childhood friends.

In school?

Yes, and our mothers were best friends.

You speak French very well. I guess you both learned French at school.

Yes.

So you came here to meet us?

Well, I promised Nabila, George's aunt, that I would come.

And George did not send anything? He never asked you anything about us?

No. Not really. George was always preoccupied with his job.

Does he know anything about us? Does he know about his father's death?

I never discussed his family with him, I said. Some things are better left alone. In our society, these are sensitive things to talk about.

You mean, having no legitimate father.

Yes.

But you knew about it, Rhea said.

It was Nabila who asked me to come here, I said, and stopped. I chewed my food slowly, delicately.

So you came to see us, with no message, Rhea insisted.

Nabila wanted Monsieur Mani to send George a French passport, I said.

Well, now, that makes a little more sense, Genevieve said. So George wants to come here?

No, it was Nabila who wanted George to come to France, I said.

But George does not want to come? Rhea asked.

I shook my head and drove the fork into my mouth. I was famished. I tried to eat slowly and with graceful manners, to use gestures that would complement the rich surroundings. But the questioning made me uncomfortable. And my laconic answers seemed to make my hosts frustrated. They hardly ate, but both sipped their wine, constantly caressing their glasses, lifting the liquid without drinking.

Suddenly, both women started to speak loud and fast and in unison.

I continued eating, and watched the maid take

the plates from beneath our noses. Rhea had a feisty presence that I liked. She was assertive, and when she talked she waved her hands or tapped them on the table. She also lifted her hair with her finger, delicately, to reveal her fair skin, her small eyes, her pointy nose. She held her fork and knife with ease, separated the vegetables from the meat, and cut them all into small pieces without piercing them with the fork. As she talked, she did not look at her mother. When they engaged in fast and sporadic conversation, like two competing monologues, the maid and I seemed irrelevant.

My eyes wandered again around the room. There was always something new to discover: framed old maps with compasses indicating north; a trace of a trip to an exotic land; African masks; a small statue of an Egyptian god; and bookshelves, coffee tables, books.

Finally, the women turned their attention back to me, and Genevieve asked me if I was planning to stay in Paris.

I am not sure.

Are you lost? she laughed.

I just got here, I said.

Rhea snapped at her mother and told her to leave me alone. *Laisse-le, putin, laisse-le!*

Now they quarrelled, and while the maid cleared the rest of the table, I stood up and walked to the window.

I looked again at the long street and could not recall if anything had changed from the last time

I had looked; through the window, everything seemed like a photo on a postcard.

Over coffee, Genevieve said that she would ask the family lawyer, Maurice, about whether they could do anything to help George. Again I felt a pang of guilt for not telling them everything I knew, but the words would not come to me.

Genevieve turned to Rhea and asked her to follow up with Maurice; she herself was leaving the next day to spend some time at their house in the south of France.

Rhea argued with her mother, calling her irresponsible.

Franchement, Genevieve said, *mais franchement*.

The women offered me cake, but I declined, thanked them, and took my leave. Rhea followed me down the stairs.

Will you come back? she asked, and her voice faintly echoed in the large void of those high walls and marble stairs.

I don't know. I am looking for a place to stay, I said.

Do you need money?

No, but I do not have the right papers to rent a room.

Well, we can take care of that, she said. Wait here. She rushed back into the apartment, picked up her bag, then followed me down the stairs and into the street. For several blocks, she held my elbow and guided me. We entered a small hotel. She booked a room under her name and paid for it. Two weeks, she told the receptionist, and turned and looked at me with a mischievous, triumphant smile.

She walked with me up the stairs to my room and stood at the door. *Voilà*, she said and kissed me on both cheeks. Then she bounced toward the stairs. On her way down, she paused and turned, smiled again, swung her hair, and said to me, You look good in my father's clothes.

I took off the clothes and laid them on the back of a chair that was tucked under a small desk. It looked like a traveller's desk, and I half-expected to see a Frenchman's hand holding a single feather and dipping the feather in a small jar of ink to carry a few drops and transform them into a flow of graceful words on elaborate yellow paper, words starting with *Ma Chère*.

I glanced at the clothes resting on the chair and wondered if there was any significance in filling one dead man's clothes with another.

I scrutinized the things in the room that seemed foreign to me: the handle that lifted the *abat-jour*, the small economical space that made the window look bigger. I lay down in the single bed next to the off-white, massive telephone that had no numbers to dial, nor rotary holes to jab your finger into. Then my curiosity took me to the bathroom, with its bidet, and tiny soap, and worn towels folded under a polite sign from the management. I stood above the toilet, undid my belt buckle, and slowly, urgently, I let the metamorphosed red wine burst and flow in the curve of a single yellow rainbow. Numbness took over my hands and my eyes and spread to my feet.

I looked out of the window and could not decide whether to go back into the streets or to lie on the bed. I opened my bag and pulled out the gun, some underwear that needed to be washed, and the wool pullover that my mother had woven for me. Every day for weeks, I remembered, she would ask me to turn my back to her, and she would paste the wool across my shoulders and run her hand along my spine, stretching the rag, ogling it from behind her myopic glasses. And she wove until she became the talk of every attic spider, every fisherman; she wove, and the wool flew to her from underneath shepherds' noses, and landed in her lap. When my pullover was done, she wove canisters, tablecloths, TV covers. She wove until she covered out whole house and surrounded me with suffocating webs.

I grabbed the keys and my bag and decided to walk around the city. As I walked, I tried to remember how to find my way back to the hotel. I noticed that the streets were wider than those in Beirut, the building facades cleaner, and the cars almost never honked. I arrived at the bank of a canal and watched the drifting boats. I sat and compared what I saw to what I had imagined from the stories about Paris my history teacher,

Mr Davidian, had told us – stories of conquests, and orders, and rolling heads from the free-falling guillotine, and the short Corsican commander who rode magnificent horses and swept through countries, escaping in a small boat from the treacherous Englishmen and their austere queens.

I walked on, and lost myself in the crowds sitting in small cafés perched on the edge of the pavement. I walked for hours, and no one looked me in the eye, though I looked directly at every single person who crossed me. I even defied some of them with my fierce look; I challenged them to the slap of a white glove on the face, hoping for a duel with the weapon of my choice. I felt secure with the weight of my gun in my bag. If I had to, I could swing the gun in any alley, through all the glimmering light, in between the tiny cars.

Now that I wore the sweater my mother had woven for me, and had left my underwear soaking in the sink, I knew I could find my gun in a second. Now I could defend this city that looked so different from the old photographs in the history books. Now I could kill Nelson, the British admiral, and become a soldier in the emperor's army. I would be the fastest shooter on a horse. I would slay priests, and hang aristocrats on trees filled with dangling biscuits. I imagined the operatic howling when I reached the palaces, imagined red-painted cheeks and fat asses under pumpkin-shaped dresses, imagined aristocrats sliding in horror and fear across endless marble floors. I listened, and contemplated the harpsichord sound of rushing sabres, the sound that would fill any revolutionary's eyes with tears of triumph.

And so I drifted for hours, trying and failing to reconcile Paris with the phantasm of my youth, with the books I had read, with my teacher's stories. And somehow, as if I had lived here once before, I traced my steps back from the sacked castles and through the glorious sites of rolling heads and falling wigs; I, a victorious soldier, returned to my small room with its small desk and scenic window view. I pulled my soaked underwear out of the sink and strangled it, and spread its wetness on the chair, over the desk, on the edge of the bed.

I did not wave a white cloth out of the window.

I slept.

CHAPTER 17

When I woke up, I felt stable, as if the sea had evaporated and the rocking had ceased.

From my window I could see the balconies on the other side of the street, smudged by fog and made wet by the Parisian rain.

I searched for a cigarette, but found that my box had been emptied last night by the aristocrats I had executed, many of whom had requested one last cigarette.

I splashed water in my eyes, freed the last few drops of wine from my belly, took a shower, brushed my teeth, and rushed down the dark stairs. I walked toward the store, and bought a Gitane Mais that had no filter. I smoked while my soldiers pulled all the jewels from the corpses, wore the aristocrats' wigs, mocked their feminine manners, frisked them for coins, bowed in front of their ladies' cadavers, swooned under their hands, and pulled off their precious rings. Before the smell of rotting powdered cheeks rose, I ordered my soldiers to burn the corpses, and when the fire roared, I walked toward the flames and lit another cigarette.

Mid-morning, the phone rang. It was Rhea. She asked me to come to the front desk.

I put on her father's clothes and went down to meet her.

When she saw me, she ran to me and kissed me for the third time since we had met. Let's go, she said.

I followed where she led. Women are part of the revolution, I thought, and one has to take what they offer.

We walked and the rain drizzled; we took shelter in a small café. Inside, I was not the only one puffing revolutionary cigarettes. We made our way through a fog of clients with newspapers that flapped like wings, rustling, toward a small, round table in the back. I ordered a coffee and croissant, which tasted of thick milk and butter. Rhea smiled at me the whole time. She looked me in the eyes like no one else had dared to.

So, can I start asking you questions? She leaned toward me in a playful manner.

Sure you can.

Tell me about George.

But before I had the chance to open my mouth, she continued, You know, I am very excited at the idea of finding my brother. I always felt alone. My father travelled all the time, and my mother was always busy with her parties and her social engagements. He is more than a security guard, isn't he? Is he really a fighter?

Yes.

Who is he fighting for?

He joined the Christian militia in East Beirut.

Tell me more.

I hesitated, not knowing where to start, or how to end. I decided to tell her stories about our school days: how George and I had always played together, about his house that was not too far from mine, about the day we crawled in the school garbage dump looking for copies of the French exam, and the day we broke into the church to steal the donation box, and the time we stole my father's car keys and drove away. I told her about the days when we began to smoke in little alleys, and how, when the war started when we were still kids, we collected empty bullets and cannon shells that we polished with lime and exchanged for cigarettes.

Rhea smiled, and when I stopped, she became like a kid at bedtime, wanting me to repeat things, to never stop. I told her that George and I had worked together, and that he decided to join the militia because he needed the money. I skipped many things about George, and when I saw how happy she was, I changed names, I planted trees, I painted the concrete houses in our old neighbourhood in tropical colours, I made people dance and laugh, even under the falling bombs.

Does he know about me? Rhea asked.

He never mentioned you, I said.

Did he ever ask about his father?

No, but when the kids at school teased him and called him 'the bastard,' he fought them no matter how big they were, he fought them until no one dared to say a word.

Was he ashamed of not having a father?

If he was, he never showed it. We never talked about it. But everyone called him George *Al-Faransawi* (George the French).

You called him that too?

No. He used his mother's family name.

What is it? Rhea tapped her cigarette.

Machrouky.

Machrouky, she repeated after me. George Machrouky. It must have hurt him to be teased like that. Kids are cruel, humans are cruel, life is cruel. She quickly drank her tea. Then she held my hand, stood up, and pulled me up with her.

Let's go. I want to show you Paris.

Rhea and I walked some more, and ended up in the Jardin du Luxembourg. The stretches of green under the many naked statues, the pigeons, and the pawns took me back to my room back home. The house must be empty now, I thought, and I wondered if Nabila had gotten the keys, if she had covered everything with drapes, if the smell of a closed, deserted home was filling the rooms, if spiders and ghosts were resting together. And I wondered if my parents, as ghosts, still had legal rights over the place, and I wondered what they would do if they came back to haunt it and discovered that I had finally succeeded in leaving and had entered those posters with the happy fountains and the pigeons, like this place here, leaving the fridge unhooked, the garbage uncollected, without a goodbye note.

On the grass I saw a partridge acting crazy with a pigeon, fighting for little breadcrumbs from under an old lady's feet. I am hungry, the partridge said, and there is nothing here for me but crumbs from a destitute hand.

We walked on, and I watched Rhea strolling next to me, telling me about the architecture, the Germans who had invaded, the little brass plates engraved with the names of French resistance fighters who had died while fighting to liberate their country. We stopped at a place that sold used books on the shore of the river, a place that I had passed the night before. Out of respect for Rhea, I ordered my soldiers to clean up the war scene and to cease all fire, theft, and disturbance. I ordered them to go underground and fight the invading fascists. My soldiers rejoiced.

After browsing in the bookstore, Rhea and I sat on a bench, watching the water slowly precipitating under the arched bridges. The stone monsters on the tops of the churches kept an eye on the enemies while my soldiers are and rested.

What do you do, Bassam? Rhea asked me.

I won't tell her of my revolutionary tendencies, nor of my crucial role in the revolution, nor of my support for the French resistance, I thought to myself and caressed my white horse. I worked at the port, I said.

And what did you do there? she asked with round, open eyes.

I drove a winch.

Your parents are still there?

They are both dead and buried underground, not too far from the undertaker's house.

When my father died, I cried for days, Rhea said. We had a distant relationship, my father and I. He was always formal, even with me, always elegant and well dressed, and he spoke like an aristocrat. (I would spare his life because he is Rhea and George's father, I thought.) He was well mannered, as all diplomats are. But he would leave us for weeks and months. At first we travelled with him, but then my mother decided to stay in Paris. She found a lover. And my father started to travel more.

George should have known him, I said.

Yes. Yes, he should have known us all, she replied quickly. Does George have a girlfriend?

No, I said.

What do you think he is doing now?

Now?

Yes, at this moment.

He is away, I said.

He is away. We know that, she giggled. Let's go and eat. You must be hungry by now. We'll take a cab.

She stepped to the edge of the street, lifted her hand in the air, stood on her toes, and spun like a ballerina, waving her palm like lovers do on a train station platform. In the cab, we sat as far as possible from each other, each next to a window. I watched Paris go by through a glass drenched by the steady rain that made everything look blurred and unknown; but Rhea, who knew the city and its people, contemplated the sopping glass and the rain droplets rushing down like tears from eyes.

In the afternoon, Rhea asked me if I wanted to come to her place for tea.

We walked through Arras Street under an umbrella that hid the tops of the high churches, the little angel statues in the eaves of buildings, the leaves of trees that bowed under the weight of the falling rain, the high, triumphant monuments, and the smoke from the ever-burning Bastille.

We left the umbrella in Rhea's hallway, dripping water, and entered her place. It was smaller than her mother's and had fewer objects. I sat and waited while she disappeared into the kitchen and then into her room. She came out wearing new, dry clothes, put on some Indian music, lit some incense, and went back into her room. After a minute she reappeared and told me to go into the kitchen and help myself to a cup of coffee. I heard a dryer blowing inside her room; outside, a storm of wind and rain rose louder, and the trees shook.

I sipped my coffee and walked over to the bookshelves in the living room. On one, I saw a photo of Rhea with a man who, I thought, must be Mr Mani. It had been taken in the Orient somewhere. A Buddhist temple filled most of the photo. It had obviously been taken from a distance, as it showed both of them in full.

Mr Mani did not look like George, except maybe for his large smile. I remembered how rare George's smiles were, how once in a while he surprised you with them, for no reason but to acknowledge your presence. Mr Mani looked Slavic, with pale skin. George had looked like his olive-skinned mother, Jamal.

That was our trip to Thailand. This is my dad, Rhea said as she approached me. She touched one side of the frame. I turned my head toward her and I kissed her on the cheek, and as I pressed my face against her warm skin, slowly she turned her head, and we kissed on the lips.

You have to take off your clothes. You are wet, Rhea murmured. Come to my room. I will give you a towel.

I stayed with Rhea for the next couple of days. We took long walks every day. We hopped from one café to another. We entered museums and galleries, and she showed me her favourite paintings. We skipped through wings filled with massive gold portraits of governors, aristocratic ladies, and white Roman statues. We went straight to her favourite pieces, and when she saw them, she rejoiced as if she had just found a lost childhood friend. She would shine a big, enthusiastic smile on me, and tell me about the painter's life, the era he had lived in, the techniques he had used, and the symbolism in his work. One day we went to a photography exhibit, and she walked calmly in front of every frame, posing in front of each photo. Photography is about death, she said to me. It preserves the illusion of a past moment that can never be re-enacted.

At night, I slept in her bed and we made love. Before going to bed, she would light a candle. I like it dark enough to see only shapes, and not too many details, she told me.

Could you describe George to me? Rhea asked one night.

In detail? I asked.

She smiled. I said, He has your green eyes and your father's smile. He is dark-skinned, more like my colour. We are almost the same height. He has straight black hair that always fell on his face. He never wore glasses. He has a hooked nose like *tante* Jamal, his mother. He is kind of skinny, but his arms have strength. You can tell by the veins that are always prominent in his arms.

Does he smoke?

Yes, he does.

What kind of cigarettes?

Marlboros.

What else does he do?

He rode a motorcycle. We went hunting together.

What did you hunt?

Birds, mostly birds.

That night, Rhea slept, but I stayed awake. I lay on my back for a while, then I walked to the window and from there to the back balcony. I smoked and looked at the few stars, and searched for the celestial bonfires, for Morse code signals from space.

After we made love, Rhea's questions would intensify. She wanted me to describe things, and she insisted on this like a neglected child. Is Beirut a big city? How do people dress? What was your mother like? Did you like your father?

Over dinner one evening, she opened wine and played French love songs. She invited me to sit on the floor next to her, and then she pulled out a photo album. Let's look at photos, she said. Slowly, she turned the pages. I looked at photos of a young infant crawling the floors, Genevieve in 1970s dresses and pointy shoes and dark sunglasses, and Rhea in her father's arms, with Africa in the background. This is my nanny, said Rhea, and that is me in Singapore. And this is at the kibbutz in Israel.

When were you there? I interrupted.

Not long ago, she said.

When I told her that George had gone there for

military training, of course Rhea wanted to know all about it.

When was he there? Why was he in Israel? And how did he manage to go from Lebanon?

I told her that George had gone on a secret mission, that he had gone to be trained.

Oh, mon Dieu, maybe we were there at the same time! Was he there in August, September, November? What year?

Last year.

Do you know where he was, what region?

No, it was supposed to be a secret training operation, I said.

Did he know that our father was Jewish? she asked.

I don't know, I said.

Do you think his mother ever discussed it? George must have asked her about his father, she added and lifted her hair from her face.

I am not sure, I replied.

The candle melted under the licks of its own flames and the flame burned over a pool of water. I stared at the fire, and my mind wandered back to the wooden benches where George and I had knelt in white robes with mumbling lips, and chewed the son of man's body, and cheerfully sipped His blood, and knew He always loved us, cannibals, petty bandits, hormonal misfits, candle thieves, and masturbators that we were.

★   ★   ★

237

The next morning, when I went back to my hotel, I took a shower and lay on my bed, looking at the ceiling, filling the room with the fog of burning cigarettes. I folded the clothes I had left strewn about and hid them in the room's small drawers. I had no plans, and I realized that I could not think of any. Other than Rhea, no one in Paris knew me, no one was expecting me for dinner, nor to walk in a funeral procession, nor to work, eat, carry the wounded, speed around on motorcycles. I could wander Paris again, I thought. Then I remembered the story of my grandmother – who in her youth was enslaved by the Turks, who in her womanhood ironed French soldiers' shirts for a few tin coins – and the story of her brother, who during the Second World War joined the six thousand Lebanese who formed the Kanasa troop, under the command of the Force Française de la Libération. I remembered my grandmother telling me of their heroic fight in the Bir Hakim battle. I remembered her telling me of her brother who perished in the desert, thirsty for his home up in the high mountains, for the chain of trees, the tolling bells, and the munching goats.

So I lit my Gitane and walked the Parisian streets looking for my ancestors' names on marble plaques, on arches of triumph. I walked like a spy in disguise, with a hat on my head, a baguette under my arm, and when I saw the Gestapo and the Vichy men rounding up thousands of people who looked like me, with the same nose and the same skin, I turned and entered the sewers. I feared being captured, I feared being cramped in trains, I feared cold nights without food, I feared being stripped of my hat, stripped of my watch, my baguette and my violin, my loved ones . . . and I also feared for the price I would pay in one way or another, in the present or in the future. I feared for the olive groves, the refugees in tents holding keys to houses they would never see again, holding photographs of the land that one day would be stolen by Slovaks in sandals with holy scripts to justify it all. I crawled the sewers until I reached the catacombs of Rome, where I rested amid the thousands of skulls lit by a small, flickering torch. Or was it the tip of my cigarette that glowed in my eyes?

The next day, Rhea came by to see me in the afternoon. She kissed me on the cheek, and as if we both knew what to do, we walked.

I asked her if she knew how her father had met George's mother.

My father, Rhea said, was a diplomat in Egypt at the time, but he left because of the Israeli-Arab War. On his way back to France, he went to Beirut to finish some business. At that time, George's mother worked as a secretary at the French consulate. My father, who was still single, young, and handsome, said he liked her accent. She must have had the same accent as you, Rhea said, smiling. George's mother was taught by nuns, but she told my father that later on she rebelled against them. I guess, after we discovered my father had cancer, he must have decided to tell me all about his life. He told me that George's mother was abused by the nuns, but nevertheless they gave her a solid education, which enabled her to land a job at the consulate. My father asked her out many times before she agreed to go out with him. Beirut . . . My father always talked about Beirut with a certain nostalgic sadness. After my father left the city, he and George's mother wrote to each other for a few weeks. Then, my father said to me, all of a sudden she stopped writing. She must have discovered that she was pregnant. For years, my father never knew of his son's existence. George's mother never told him, nor did my father suspect anything. It was only after many years that he was travelling in Rome and met a Lebanese business-man who happened to know the family, and this man told my father that George's mother had become pregnant by a French man who had left the country, and that she had decided to keep the baby in spite of all the social taboos, the hardship she had to face, the church's excommunication threats, and the isolation she faced from her family and society. I asked my father why he never went back to Beirut to see George and his mother. He said that after the war started, Beirut became dangerous for people like him.

Rhea looked me again in the eye. George's mother was defiant, wasn't she?

She was also generous, I said, and she loved us both.

How did she die?

From the same disease as your father.

And maybe at the same time, Rhea added.

CHAPTER 18

For two days after our conversation about her father and George's mother, Rhea did not call and did not show up at the hotel. On the second night, I walked to her place. I stood across from her building at the intersection of two streets, under the traffic signal. I inhaled at the yellow light and released white fumes on the green. When the light turned red, I stood among the gathered pedestrians and observed their colourful clothes.

I saw a well-dressed older man waiting at the entrance to Rhea's building. I watched the street-light projecting beams on his face, and saw that he changed colours like a chameleon. Then I saw Rhea come down. I retreated from the corner and stood in the shadows. Rhea kissed the older man, and they walked together down the street. He was skinny, and delicate-looking, with a baby face. I followed them, keeping to the shadows; when they looked behind them, I froze like prey in the presence of a predator.

Rhea and the man entered a bar. He opened the door for her. On the way to the bar she had done all the talking; he just nodded and leaned his head toward her.

I waited outside the bar. I smoked all my cigarettes, and still I stood, watching through the windows. The waitresses walked back and forth, blocking the central light that was suspended in the middle of the window frame like an extraterrestrial ship. At times, the waitresses' movements made the light flicker in my eyes. I thought of these flickers as Morse code signals instructing me not to lose my subjects, to follow their tracks, to take note of every laugh and every conversation, no matter how trivial, to watch their body gestures, to detect any exchange of paper, cigarette boxes, glances, smiles, tender voices.

I waited for hours on end. I craved another cigarette, and I also craved the burning candles above Rhea's bed. I craved her photos, her endless questions.

When Rhea and the man finally left the bar, I froze. I did not blink. The man stopped onto the sidewalk and pulled out a box of cigarettes and an old lighter. Then he lit a smoke, puffed, and walked beside Rhea. I followed them as they traced back their route to Rhea's home. The man walked her to the door, she kissed him, and he left on foot. I waited until he passed me, and then I followed him down to the metro. I stood on the platform, not too far from him. I watched him closely. The suspended neon light gave him disturbing shadows that were at odds with his blue eyes, his silk tie, and his well-combed hair.

I got on and off at every station he did; I followed him everywhere, and I did not care whether he noticed it or not.

When he got off at the last station and began to walk away, I ran after him. In a little *ruelle*, I asked him for a cigarette. He answered rudely, saying that he did not have any.

I know you have one! I replied.

He brushed past me with an air of arrogance and told me to scram.

I pulled out my gun and rushed in front of him. Either the cigarette, or I will use the gun. Which would you prefer?

He pulled the box from the side pocket of his jacket and gave it to me.

The lighter too, I said.

He frisked his clothes, pulled the lighter from a pants pocket, and gave it to me slowly, still looking at me with fearless eyes. I took it and walked away in the opposite direction. I decided not to take the metro in case the man called the police; they would surely keep an eye on the stations.

I walked fast through deserted streets, and I felt my hunger. I had not eaten all day because I had been waiting for Rhea to call, waiting to share food with her, to look at her looking at me straight in the eyes like no one ever looked at you in this city, to smell her hair.

When I finally arrived on a busy street, I stood

behind a young tree and lit a cigarette. I felt the weight of the lighter and examined its gold colour. It had some initials that I decided to examine later under better light. I opened and closed it; when it closed, it snapped and gave a sound that echoed like a jail door, like the clang of a torture chamber, like lovers quarrelling in cars and parking lots, like my father's exist from our home at night and his exits from gambling joints in the morning. I was thirsty, but the thought of water brought back the memory of Rambo's hand on my neck, drowning me, and the thought cut the air from my chest, which made me inhale my cigarettes longer and walk faster, and the faster I walked the more like a stranger I felt. I longed for my lengthy walks under falling bombs. Bombs are not only for killing, I thought; bombs are like Morse code signals filled with messages, with words. But Paris has no falling bombs; Paris is a mute city.

The next day, Rhea phoned from the lobby of my hotel.

She said that she was coming up to my room. When she entered, she slammed the door (like the slam of an expensive gold lighter).

You followed me last night, she accused me.

I kept quiet.

Yes, you did. I saw you. I saw you waiting outside the bar, across the street. I recognized your posture, your bag, your cigarettes. You stood there for hours, like a stalker. I recognized you from the way you smoked and the way you looked sideways from under your hat and coat collar. Yes, you stood under the dim light, thinking no one could recognize you, but I always recognize people by their shapes. I prolonged my stay in the bar because I did not want to leave before you, but stubborn as you are, you stood there as if someone had paid you. You stood there, and the look of your stiff, sad body, like a standing corpse, terrified me. What right do you have? What right do you have to follow me? I saw you following Roland after he left me. I saw you! she shouted. Why did you follow him? What right?

Her eyes looked straight at me again, but this time it was a new look that I had never seen before, a kind of a squint like that of a marksman shooting against the sun, the squint of a lost sailor, the squint of a person looking through smoke from a cigarette or burning hay.

Why, why? Now, tell me why you followed me. Why? she shouted.

To protect you, I mumbled.

What? To protect me? From what, from whom? Who asked you to? Who? You have no claim on me, do you understand? I took pity on you, and just because I felt sorry for you and slept with you, you do not own me. Understood? Now, do not ever follow me again! She raised her finger to my face and said, And do not bother Roland, because he is not as soft and fragile as you think.

She turned and slammed the door (yes, it

sounded like a prison door). From my window, I watched her crossing the street, stepping over the white interrupted traffic line, and disappearing behind white stone walls.

I paced my room between the window and the bathroom, looking for something new, something to examine. I was missing soap and needed a new towel. I went downstairs to the lobby.

The receptionist, an Algerian man with thick glasses and curly hair, was reading a book. Slowly, he lifted his head. When I asked for a new towel and soap, he told me that I would have to wait until the next cleaning. I asked him if he had a book I could borrow.

He leaned under the desk and pulled out a few books. Here, he said. People forget books in their rooms and we keep them. Like a juggler, he held a wobbling pile of books in his hand and put them all in front of me. Choose. We expect you to bring them back when you finish them or before you leave.

I picked *L'Étranger* by Camus.

Ah oui. On est tous ça ici, mon frère, he said and laughed.

I went up to the room and lay in bed. *Mother died today. Or maybe yesterday; I can't be sure.* This was the first sentence in the book. I got up and sat at the window and flipped through the pages in the book. When I glanced down at the street, I saw a man and his dog walking. The man cursed his dog. The sun shone strong and low, which made Paris slide into Mediterranean heat. The smell of thyme filled the cafés, and the stronger the sun poured down its heat, the more Paris slid toward the North African shores. Between the covers of my book, I saw the protagonist walking on the seashore with a gun in his hand . . . *This man who is morally guilty of his mother's death*, the prosecutor said and pointed at the accused. I quickly left the courtroom and dropped the book on the bed to watch Paris continue its path downward and south under glittering red waves of light. Reflections of desert sand joined to waves of water from the Mediterranean Sea. The heat was so great it made me dizzy, and I felt myself perspiring through my back in a cascade of sweat that rushed down my pants and crossed my buttocks. I felt its dampness on the joints behind my knees.

I rushed to my bed and fell onto it, feeling sick and deeply anxious. I reached for the phone and lifted the receiver. The Arab downstairs answered me.

Do you have vinegar? I asked him. I wanted to wet a piece of cloth with vinegar and lay it on my forehead, just as my grandmother had done when I was young and had a deadly fever.

Vinegar? he repeated. This is a hotel. We do not have vinegar.

Khall, I said.

The receptionist hung up. I threw the phone on the floor and walked toward the bathroom. There, I peeked out the window: outside, the sand was blowing spray like crashing sea waves at docks and ports. Far away in the desert I saw Rommel and his men moving toward the east. I held my gun and dug under the window, and waited for their passage.

The partridge flew down and landed on the windowsill. *I will tell you when they pass*, it told me.

I woke up a while later, not knowing what time it was. My shirt was soaked. A desert thirst made me rush to the bathroom. I filled a glass from the well and drank. I looked in the mirror: my hair was wet and my body was skinny; my round eyes were red and sunk beneath the yellow skin of my high cheekbones. My clothes were covered in dust. I must have crawled in the boiling sand, I thought, under the enemy's eyes. I must have escaped from beneath my enemy's long leather boots.

I took a shower, and under the water I felt my forehead. The fever had gone. When I got out of the shower, I looked for my watch. It was four in the afternoon, but that did not help me much because I could not remember when, exactly, Paris had started to move south, or when it had finally deserted its colonies and slid back north.

I called the Algerian downstairs and asked him if he remembered what day it had been when I asked for vinegar. He laughed and did not answer the question. Instead, he asked me if I had finished my book.

No, I said.

★   ★   ★

Mother died today. Or maybe yesterday; I can't be sure.

The first sentence of the book played in my head again and again until I started to laugh at its absurdity. I laughed at the memory of my mother's distant cousin, who had come from the north dressed all in black, and in a melodramatic act of lamentation had thrown herself on my mother's open coffin and had a conversation with her. She had told my mother that her son, Bassam, was still here, but was alone now, and she had reminded my mother how young she was for death, which made all the women in black shriek and shed tears in their handkerchiefs. The image of women surrounding my mother's corpse, dressed all in black, all in tears, all sipping coffee, all kissing me on the forehead, all chanting and beating their chests, made me want to laugh even more. And I remembered Father Semaan, the bearded, short, fat priest who came to my room swinging his incense on my teenager's posters of half-naked girls and football players, and also on the pigeons outside my window, who, when they saw his fire and smoke, flew up in flocks and perched on the opposite roof, ogling him cock-eyed. All I had wanted was for the crowd to leave the house. I had not been certain about when my mother had died – whether it was today or yesterday or even the day before. And here they were, these women, talking to her as if she were still there and listening. They helped themselves to the kitchen coffee and the cigarettes, and opened the fridge, hoping for cold water, reviving one another with rosewater, fainting like Italian opera singers, wailing. And all I saw that day of my mother's funeral was a black drape stretched over many tearful heads, all bound under one black sheet, moving in agony like a swaying, injured beast. Then the men came and made their way through the women's black robes, lifting the coffin with twelve arms, and my mother floated her way to the cemetery along streets filled with cars and nosy neighbours perched on balconies like half-vulture, half-human beings with curved claws. I had walked in the procession and looked at the wreaths with white ribbons across their middles, with their dedications and mourners' names. I had walked, and when I realized that someone was holding my arm for fear that I might faint, slip, or crawl behind the coffin, I had looked that person in the eye and asked for a cigarette.

In Paris, the soft evening light crawled along the surface of the sidewalks, and a breeze rose outside, and up wafted the smell of the freshly wet streets. I opened a drawer, pulled out an envelope, and counted my money. I might have enough for another week, maybe more, I thought. The room was rented for a few more days, but I did not expect Rhea to renew it.

I took my money and went downstairs. The Algerian had left, and another man, a Senegalese, was sitting in his place. I asked him to extend my stay for another week, under the same name.

Who is Rhea? he asked. The room is under Rhea Mani's name.

My girlfriend, I said.

He nodded, asked nothing more, and filled out some papers. I paid him and left. Outside, I went searching for food. The shadows of lamp poles were reflected on the wet streets in obscure shapes; they looked like serpentine ghosts in trench coats, with burning hair.

I bought a baguette with a *saucisse* inside. Then I walked to the river, leaned on the rail, and buried the baguette in my stomach.

The palaces across the river were lit with green and red lights. Above, foggy weather brought the sky lower and made the city look confined and humble.

I took the steps down to the river's edge and sat on a bench and waited for the fog to descend and touch the water.

Now, I thought, all is invisible; all is hidden from laws, eyes, perception. This must be death, where nothing is seen.

I wore the fog as a garment and walked with it into the night.

The next day, the phone rang. The Algerian said, *Une nana t'attend en bas. Elle veut que tu descendes.*

I knew it was Rhea. I put her father's pants on and ran barefoot down the stairs. She was in the lobby, talking to the man I had mugged a couple of nights before. They both looked at me in silence, then looked at each other.

Do you have time to come for a coffee with us? Rhea asked in a brisk, businesslike tone.

Yes, I will be right back, I replied.

I put on my socks and shoes, and her father's shirt, which I had washed but had not ironed. Outside the hotel, the man stared at me in silence, with an expressionless face. We walked together to a café and sat down.

Rhea gave me a reproving look, and with a tight jaw, she said, Do you have Roland's lighter?

I pulled it from my pocket and gave it back to him.

And the gun? Where did you get the gun? she asked.

Beirut.

You entered the country with a gun? Roland asked with a smirk on his face.

Yes, I did.

Carrying a gun in this country is a serious matter, Roland said.

I shrugged my shoulders.

Rhea squeezed my arm from across the table and said forcefully, You listen to him, Bassam. Roland knows what he is talking about! Listen to him.

Roland looked around, as if informers were surrounding us. He said, You have to get rid of it. Do you have it now in your bag?

Yes, I do.

C'est pas vrai! Rhea shouted. She pulled her upper body back and slammed her hand on the little round table. *Mais, c'est ridicule, non?*

Go tonight and throw it in the river, Roland whispered to me.

Listen to him, Rhea said again. Listen to him. He knows.

Go throw it in the river and all is forgiven, Roland said. He went to the counter and paid the bill.

Rhea looked down at her fingernails. She avoided my eyes, and her soft hair veiled her face. All around us mutters, whispers, and murmurs blended with the clatter of utensils, cigarette smoke that escaped lovers' sighs, and soft, sad, singing accordions that accompanied our uneasiness and silence.

When Roland came back, Rhea stood up and grabbed her large bag. On his way out, Roland pushed a box of cigarettes toward me. Here, keep this; it might make you refrain from future heroic acts.

I pushed it back toward him. When I need something, I will take it myself, I said.

I stayed in the café for a while and drank the mineral water that Rhea had ordered and never touched.

When I left, I walked through the streets of Paris, and the weight of the gun in my bag was heavier than before. I wondered if I would walk the same way with no weight on my back. I wondered if I would feel naked. What would the emperor think if I laid down my arms in the river? It must be a conspiracy, I thought; Roland is a rich aristocrat, and if I lose my gun it will only serve the purpose of vanity, heredity, and oppression.

I went back to my room and waited for the sun to sink into the water, and for the water to rise and fill the earth, and swallow all the rivers and streams. I was horizontal, in bed, flowing perfectly parallel to the low ceiling. I held my gun and extended my arm. I aimed at the painting on the wall of deer hunters and dogs sniffing the ground.

Then I aimed the gun at myself and looked the barrel in the face. If I possessed the baccarat kind of gun instead of an automatic, would I play with my fate? Would I leave myself only one bullet and roll the barrel, like so many young men had in Beirut during the war, after watching the movie *The Deer Hunter*? Many had died playing De Niro's game. A few of us knew that Roger, the son of Miriam the widow, had pulled the trigger one night, and the blood from his brain had stained the cocaine on the table, and George's shirt, and Issam's face, and my chest. We had carried him down the stairs, Issam and I, and laid him in the back seat of his car. It is no use blocking the flow of blood, George said to me. He is gone. When we arrived at the hospital, we waited in the hallway

255

and smoked, without remorse. We smoked until the paramedic came out and asked us for the dead man's name and the story of what had happened. George told him that Roger was shot while fighting at the *jabhah*. The paramedic did not buy the story. He smelled the lies in our silk shirts and in our cologne that overwhelmed the smell of blood. He looked at us with suspicious eyes and mumbled hesitantly, *It is a very close-range bullet*. George pulled the paramedic to one side, put his hand on the man's shoulder, talked in his ear, slipped his hand higher to his neck, and talked to him some more. He released the paramedic with a push. The man walked back in anger, taking off his medical coat and throwing it in protest on a rolling stretcher, cursing the war, his job, the gods, and his land of madness.

At the funeral, Zaghlloul had sung *Zajal*, and the men had danced with the coffin. Roger's mother walked the streets shouting to the balconies, He is a hero, my son is a hero, I gave birth to a *batal, batal*.

When night came to Paris again, I went to face the river. I cursed all the rivers from Jordan to the Mississippi. I stood at the water's edge, and held my bag, and opened its zipper. Treacherous rivers that wash you and leave you naked and cold, I shouted. I pulled out the gun, but did not throw it.

I walked back to the hotel. On the way, I stopped

at a store and bought plastic bags and a rope. I went to my room and wrapped the gun in many bags, and tightened the bundle with ropes and knots. Then I walked again to the river, to its most deserted point. I found an old, rusty bridge there; it stood alone, with no one to witness its darkness. I walked under it, and there I saw traces of homelessness and small fires. I tightened the end of the rope to the beam of the bridge, and I threw the gun into the river. It sunk, and as it sunk it joined the rusty cannon ball, the thirsty dead soldiers, and the emperor's horses that grazed underneath the river's banks.

I walked back to the hotel feeling an unbearable lightness. The bag on my back seemed irrelevant, useless, the echo of a large insect buzzing below my ear.

In my room, I found that my bed had been made. The bathroom contained a fresh wave of new soaps and a clean towel. The toilet paper was rolled and pleated at the tip.

I opened the window and let air in. The drizzle from the shower fell on my foaming body parts. When I stopped the water, I plucked the towel and swept my body with it.

Wearing only my underwear, I reached for my book. I opened it: . . . *and has the uttered a word of regret for his most odious crime?*

No, I answered. Why should he? We all agreed to participate. It was our choice, we each spun our own gun barrels, we each had four chances

257

out of five. We all acted out of our own convictions, and out of passion. Reason? you ask. Mr Prosecutor, while we are all sweating in this courtroom filled with French men and judges, reason is a useful fiction.

I left the court, and turned another page in my book: . . . *but all this excitement exhausted me and I dropped heavily onto my sleeping-plank.*

CHAPTER 19

In the morning, the phone rang.

It is Roland, the voice on the other end of the line said.

Yes.

We should meet, but come without your object.

It is in the river.

Oh good, good, excellent. Then come by this afternoon. We need to talk. I will meet you at four at the Montparnasse metro.

I went downstairs and out to buy a coffee.

Hakim (I had discovered that was the name of the Algerian) asked me if I had finished my book.

Yes, I said, but I am keeping it.

He laughed and said, You might have to pay a price for your deeds.

But I am willing.

Roland met me at the metro station. He was, as usual, well dressed, well combed, and smelled of cologne. We exited the station, and I got into his Renault.

Are you hungry? Roland asked.

Yes.

Good. Come to my place and I will make you a small dinner.

Roland's apartment was filled with tableaux, artifacts, and rugs. From a large, open window there was a view of the Eiffel Tower. Roland opened a bottle of wine from his modest wine cellar and poured the whole bottle into a decanter. Then, after a few minutes, he poured me a glass.

Is Rhea coming? I asked after the second sip.

No, she is not.

She is upset?

Yes, she is upset, but she also wants to help. Rhea is not for you. You have different lives.

Why does she still want to help? I asked.

Rhea has convictions and religious beliefs. She also considers you to be the closest thing to her brother. When you followed us that night, Roland said as he poured oil into a pan, we were discussing the possibility of bringing George here to Paris. Rhea is concerned about her brother. Though she has never met him, still her curiosity is slowly turning to some kind of . . . how should I say it? Not love, but maybe obsession, if you ask me.

It is normal, no? I said.

Normal to be infatuated with someone you've never met? I do not know. But I do understand, because maybe she feels she is alone, without a family.

What is your last name? I said.

My last name? He seemed surprised. Meusiklié.

260

The lighter was not yours, I said. The initials do not match your name.

It belonged to Claude, Rhea's father.

He gave it to you.

No. I kept it after he died.

You were close?

Actually, we worked together.

Diplomats?

Yes, diplomats, Roland laughed.

Why are you laughing? I asked.

Rhea calls us spies.

Are you?

Well, maybe to some extent all diplomats are spies.

So, why did you invite me here?

Rhea asked me to help you. I was reluctant at first, but Rhea insisted. You have to leave France. You have no papers, and you will not get any for years to come, and the police will catch up with you sooner or later. You have no money, I assume, or you would not have been so desperate for cigarettes, if you know what I mean.

Roland winked at me. So, my dear little man, here is what I suggest to you. I hope you like *escargots à la sauce au basilic? Bref*, here is what I suggest to you. More wine?

He poured himself some more wine, chopped some parsley, then turned and washed his hands. Well, like I said . . . Bring your glass here . . . Here is what I suggest. Canada.

Canada, I repeated.

Yes. You call this man who knows someone, who knows someone else, who can get you a fake visa to Canada.

Now you are talking like a spy, I said.

Perceptive. Indeed, you are one perceptive young man. Did you come with a passport or just guns? Roland smiled.

Yes, a passport.

Good, not so irresponsible after all. You get on the plane, and when you arrive at the Montreal airport in Canada, you claim refugee status. I will give you the number of the person later. Rhea said she would pay for it all – the ticket and the other fees. She will contact you about it. Now, let's eat. Oh, by the way, he added, did you happen to see George before you left?

No, I said.

Roland shook his head and led me to my seat at the table.

The next morning, I went to a public telephone booth.

I called the number Roland had given me. A woman answered. I told her that I was calling about the suit for the wedding that was taking place outside the city.

What is the colour and size of the suit? she asked.

It is blue, and the size is seven.

Good. Where can we meet? she said.

Metro Montparnasse. I will be wearing a white shirt with long sleeves that cover my hands.

Tomorrow morning at eight-thirty, she said. I will find you.

After I hung up, I strolled to a nearby café and ordered a cup of coffee. The waiter was polite and called me *Monsieur*. I opened a newspaper and went through it slowly.

There was news about a car bomb that had exploded in East Beirut, killing five people and injuring thirty. The photograph showed a woman covered with blood being rushed to an ambulance.

I moved closer to the café window and stared at the photograph. I tried to see if I could recognize the woman or anyone else in the photo. The caption read 'Achrafieh,' which was where I had lived. The ground was covered with glass and rubble, and in the background a man pointed to the balcony above him. The article in the paper was disconcertingly factual, without story or investigation.

Try as I might, I could not recognize anyone in the photo. So I sipped my coffee, and when the waiter was looking away, I carefully ripped out the page, folded it with my hands under the table, and put it in my pocket.

I made my way back to my hotel and up to my room. There, I pulled the page from my pocket and laid it on the desk. Then I lay in bed and looked at the walls. After a while, I picked up my book. I was on the last few pages. I read, *I informed him that I'd been staring at the walls for months, there was nobody, nothing in the world . . . A life which*

I can remember, this life on earth. That is all I want from it.

I closed the book and looked at the sun, which had come into the room like melancholy consolation.

That afternoon, I walked to Rhea's place and waited near her building. I did not ring the bell, but I did make myself conspicuous. I stood in the light. I fretted like the leaves. I smoked, and puffed Native Indian signals, sending her a warning of my coming.

Soon I saw Rhea's long coat and umbrella sliding above the sidewalks, slowly approaching me, slowly becoming bigger. She saw me, passed me, avoided my look, and went straight to her door.

I approached her and slipped under her umbrella. I talked to Roland, I said to her from under the rain.

Good. Now you can leave.

You want me to leave?

Look, what you did was unforgivable and, to tell you the truth, a little scary. Roland did not want to help at first. I asked him to.

Why are you helping me?

I am doing it for George.

She opened the door to her building, and before she could close it, I held on to the side of it and asked her if I could come in.

She did not answer, so I followed her inside. In the elevator she did not say a word; instead, she looked at her shoes the whole time. Her shoes were shiny black, flat and round, with a little heel, and the rain had beaded on them. I followed her shoes down the long hallway. I followed her black leather shoes like a wet puppy – one of those poodles that fill Paris's streets with their leashes that expand like spider strings from their owners' hands.

Rhea opened the apartment door and threw her keys in a bowl. She went to her room and closed the door behind her. Then she came back out and asked me if I was hungry.

No, I said.

Did you call the people?

Yes.

Good, so you decided.

No, but I did call them.

You have no future here; you have to leave.

I held her hand and drew her close to me. She tried to pull away, but I held her firm. She hid her face from me, veiling it with her soft hair. I lifted her hair slowly, and I caressed her face. She stood there, motionless, hesitant. I kissed her on the cheek, then on the neck. When I reached her lips, she kept them closed.

You are wet, she said. You'd better go home and change your clothes. She gently pushed me away. Call me when you get the visa. I will book the ticket.

I left her apartment and retraced my poodle-wet tracks along the hallway. When I looked back,

I saw she was watching me from a small opening in her doorway.

The next day, I stood at the Montparnasse metro entrance. A woman in her forties pulled at my long sleeves and smiled. She walked ahead of me, and I followed her. We ended up in a small park with a few benches. She sat down and looked me in the face.

When did you get here?

A few weeks ago.

She nodded. From where?

Lebanon.

The situation is bad there, she said in an accent I could not recognize. Why did you leave?

I am not welcome there any more.

Not welcomed by whom?

By the people in power.

Could you be less vague, please?

You need the story? I asked. I was accused of killing someone, but I did not do it. I was tortured.

Did you go through a trial?

No.

Who tortured you?

The militia.

Why?

Like I said, because they accused me of stealing, and of killing someone!

You said killing first. You did not say stealing.

Well, that too.

Tell me more about the torture. Were you

tortured alone, or with a friend, or someone from your family?

Alone.

How?

I told the woman about Rambo. About the water bath, and how he dipped my head in it, and how he would pull it back just before I suffocated. I told her about the sleep deprivation, the car trips, and the long interrogations.

And why do you think they chose you?

I was singled out because I smoke drugs, and I believe also because the leader knew my uncle was a communist.

The woman asked me many questions. She wanted details, like my full name, my age, and when exactly I had left.

The reason I asked to meet, she said, is first because I need your passport, and second just so that you know we do not do this for profit. We do it only for people who are refugees. We are an underground humanitarian organization. Do you understand that?

Yes, I said.

Good. Do you have your passport on you?

Yes.

Good.

You see the taxi there?

The small white car? I asked.

Yes.

After I leave, you take that car and let the driver take you home. Leave him your passport. We will let you know when the visa is done. And please do not try to make conversation with the driver, and do not call the number again. Avoid policemen and crowded public places. Do not get arrested. We will reach you when everything is done.

I took the taxi. On the way, I threw the passport on the passenger seat. When we arrived at my hotel, I said, This is where I am staying.

The driver asked me for the fare.

Two days passed, and I did not attempt to see Rhea. I had finished reading my book. I slipped it in my bag, hoping to regain some of the weight. I had lost in the absence of my gun.

One clear night, I walked back to the spot where I knew my gun lay. I hoped that the gun might have resurfaced and was floating against the current. Or maybe it was in the possession of a dead, underwater French soldier. Maybe it was using its own speed, accuracy, and semi-automatic capacity to shoot all the passing *mouche* boats from underneath, and sink the American agents on the boats posing as tourists and wine connoisseurs.

I stood for a minute, watching for bubbles, and hoping again for the gun to bounce up from under the water like fish that jump to chase hovering, narcissistic flies, gazing at their own reflection above the mirrored river surface. But the water was still. Then I heard gunshots muffled by the current of the river, and I knew that someone had unwrapped my gun. I approached the bank carefully, leaned over its edge, and saw the shifting shapes of the castles above me, and my own reflection. And my eyes beamed battle scenes from Beirut: I saw myself as a kid, running behind Al-Woutwat, who was using his AK-47 to shoot from behind sandbags; and I saw my little hands running after warm, empty bullets and collecting them in my shirt, in a kangaroo-pouch shape. And I saw the joy in my face while hopping (like a kangaroo) back home, and later exchanging my treasure with the neighbourhood kids.

For two more days, I did not hear from Rhea or the visa lady. The first morning, I took the metro and walked to the Eiffel Tower. Tourists like little ants strolled under the monster's metal feet. They looked up at it, protecting their eyes with small plastic cameras, posing underneath it like smiling statues, pressing their index fingers on tiny buttons to suck the light from their smiling faces, and to record the passing of time in latent images that were proof of their existence and the impermanence of their lives.

I sat and watched the pigeons feeding on sugary crumbs that fell from the children's lips. I saw tourists landing in their buses, bouncing like astronauts, with bags filled with maps and guidebooks that might give them clues to the mystery of the moon. Those books talked about the importance of choosing the right restaurants and gave directions to the right museums, where the residues of history and the theft of empires were boxed in glass menageries suitable for their visits in the morning after tiny French breakfasts, which they ate while feeling nostalgic for lines at the buffet, and long stainless-steel containers, and wrinkled eggs, and over-easy eggs, and tasteless potato chunks, and neon-coloured jams, and chewy Wonderbread, and diluted coffee, which they sipped in sync with the big band music that filtered through from the kitchen, spiced by the humming of the black cook behind the swinging doors with the round boat windows that also swing on the Mississippi in ships that carry the tourists' flour, corn, and greasy bacon.

The second morning, I stayed in bed, and Paris stood still and did not move or shift. I waited for the scenery to change outside my window, but it remained the same.

Down the street, a trail of soldiers returning from battle called me to march. So eventually I got up and marched to the Arc de Triomphe. I crossed the wide street swamped by impatient cars, running in circles. I passed under the arc and declared my triumph over my enemies. When I crossed to the other side, I decided to eat. I roamed the city looking for food. I sat at a café table and watched all the people rushing along the sidewalks. I ate what I was offered, paid, and walked back to my hotel.

Hakim at the front desk had a message for me: My suit was ready, and I was to come and pick it up tomorrow at the same hour, the same place.

That night, I had the urge to see Rhea. I walked to her place, and from far across the street I watched her bedroom. Her light was on, and every time her shadow brushed the window I would hide behind the wall, erasing my shape.

I watched her room until I ran out of smokes.

The third morning, I met the visa lady. We walked to the park where we'd talked before. We sat on the same bench.

We have it, she said. Here is what you should do. In the plane, before you arrive in Montreal, you go to the bathroom. You tear up your passport and dump it in the toilet. Do not leave a trace of it. Then, when you get off the plane, you tell the officer that you want to ask for refugee status. Make sure you tear up the passport. Do you have any other identification on you?

Yes, a Lebanese birth certificate.

That you can keep. Now tonight, go to this address. It is a restaurant. Someone will come and give the passport to you there. Be there around eight in the evening. Good luck.

I watched the woman leaving. I watched her rushing through the crowd, melting with the coats and suitcases, never to be seen again.

★   ★   ★

In the evening, I went to the restaurant. I ordered a beer, and smoked, and contemplated the night, like the Parisians do.

The place had small, round tables, crowded one next to the other, and everyone in haled everyone else's smoke. The round tables in such close proximity to one another formed a series of over-lapping circles. Occasionally the formation was cut by the waiter's white apron, crossing through and between tables like scissors. I waited, and after an hour I started to get nervous. No one had approached me, nor had I talked to anyone except the waiter. Finally, the waiter came to give me the bill, leaned against me, and said, *C'est déjà dans ta poche*.

I walked outside and frisked my pockets. I felt the passport in one of them.

Now I am allowed to fly, I thought. So I flew over Paris, watching the citizens' hats bobbing like moving targets, the dogs sniffing one another's wet tails, headlights going in circles and chasing one another like the dogs. And the higher I flew, the smaller the people became, smaller and smaller, minuscule and insignificant, and the more the streets and houses were arranged in circles, cut and shaped like tables around which brooding artists puffed their cigarettes and contributed to the evolution of the thick Parisian fog that concealed their deep thoughts from flying humans and sniffing dogs.

When I landed, I passed the Senegalese concierge at the hotel desk, forgot to greet him, and ran straight up to my room. I opened my passport: A Canadian visa was stamped in it.

CHAPTER 20

The next morning, I woke up early, rushed to Rhea's apartment building, and rang her bell. Her sleepy voice came through the intercom.

I have the visa, I said.

Tu veux du café? she asked.

Oui, I answered.

She buzzed me up, and I found her walking slowly around her kitchen. Her nightgown was thin, white, transparent. She must have felt my eyes penetrating her short robe because she looked back at me and caught me staring. She quietly went to her room, changed into regular clothes, then came back and sat facing me. What are you doing these days? she asked.

I am reading and walking, I said.

She nodded. What are you reading?

A story about someone who kills an Arab in Algeria.

L'Étranger? she asked.

Oui, c'est ça.

She smiled. Come, let's sit on the balcony, she said. It will be a few days before we get the air ticket. I will check today with Monique, the travel agent. Are you going to keep out of trouble until then? I do not appreciate being stalked.

I finished my cigarette.

I would like to sleep with you again, I said.

Maybe, just before you leave, Rhea said. Not today or tomorrow, but maybe the night before your departure. There is a party tonight over at the house of some of my friends. You can come if you promise to behave and ask for what you need politely.

That evening, I went again to Rhea's place. Together we took a taxi and went to a party in a long loft containing a few red hallway lights and fuzzy purple sofas. The entranceway was filled with a blasé crowd, the kind that intently ignores your passage, like houseplants in permanent poses. Painted-hair owners and tight-leather-pant fillers danced in a corner, using moonwalk moves. Rhea disappeared, and I stood against a wall holding a bottle of beer in my hand. I watched the purses, the high, thin heels, the black lace stockings, and the flamboyant hairstyles of the women.

After a while, I spotted Rhea talking to a man, and then he followed her up a set of stairs. She led, and the man walked behind her, swaying to the loud music.

A man with black lipstick on his lips and wild hair approached me. Hey, *t'es l'ami de Rhea*?

Yes, I answered.

I am her *coiffeur*, he said.

And her mother's, I presume?

Bien oui, je connais la connasse, he laughed, rocking his thin, silky body back and forth.

What is upstairs? I asked.

Ah, this is the place to go up, up, he answered and looked at the ceiling.

I finished my beer and walked farther inside the loft. Everyone here affected a nonchalant air of importance, a kind of modern pseudo-aristocratic persona. If only I had my gun, I thought sadly, I would shoot them on the steps of their palaces.

Half an hour later, I was bored with the collective act of coolness, the languid conversations, the statuesque poses. I grabbed hold of the *coiffeur* and said to him, Listen, could you go up and tell Rhea that I am leaving?

And what do I get if I do this? he smiled and put his hands on his hips.

Nothing, absolutely nothing. You get to do me a favour only, I said, and I might not spear your head when the revolution arrives.

I will do it for your accent, and your wide eyes, and long, long lashes, the *coiffeur* replied and swiftly turned and climbed the stairs gracefully, like a lama.

I could not find her, he said when he returned. Jinni said that she must have left.

I went downstairs and into the street, and there I saw Rhea talking to the same man she had been with inside. There was tension between them;

Rhea looked agitated, and the man looked angry. I waited and observed from afar. Suddenly, the man grabbed Rhea's arm and dragged her toward a car.

I ran over and pushed him away from her.

Rhea started to cry. The man pulled a knife from his pocket and brandished it at me. Rhea ran to him and begged, *Non, Moshe. Arrête! C'est un ami à moi.*

Go away, Bassam! she shouted at me. Why are you following me?

I stood still.

Rhea held the man's arm. *Va t'en!* she kept screaming at me. Then she opened the car door and said to the man, *Bien voilà*, I will come with you.

The man shoved her in the car and walked to the driver's side. I will take care of you later, he said, pointing his finger at me. He drove away.

I memorized the car's plate number and went back to the party, reciting the number like a mantra. I sought out the *coiffeur*, snatched his bag, pulled out his kohl pencil, and quickly wrote the number on the wall. Then I asked him if he would find me some paper. He disappeared and came back with an empty box of cigarettes. I tore it up and wrote the number on it.

As I left for good, the *coiffeur* asked me if I would not write down his number as well.

Putain de macho! he shouted after me, and his words echoed down the spiral stairs.

On the way back to my hotel, the idea of calling Roland came to me. Perhaps he could help Rhea. I called him from my room and woke him up. I told him the story.

It is better not to interfere, Roland said and hung up on me.

By noon the next day, I was still in bed. I had called Rhea in the morning, but no one had answered.

Finally, in the afternoon, I went to the desk downstairs. Hakim, I said, you are my friend, no?

Hakim laughed and said, What do you need?

Just a small question. Could you find out the address and name of someone from their car's licence plate?

Leave me the number. It might cost you some-thing, he said.

How much?

Later, he smiled. I will see what I can do for the brother.

I called Rhea again, and this time she answered.

I am coming to see you, I said.

No! she shouted.

I am coming to see you, I repeated.

No, she said. I will not open the door.

I walked to her building and buzzed the intercom. She answered, Go away!

I held my finger on the buzzer.

Then, through the glass of the thick door, I saw

an old lady with two tiny sausagelike dogs coming toward me from the elevator. I walked to the door, and when she opened it, I said with utmost politeness, *Laisse-moi vous aider, madame.*

I held the door for the old lady and entered the building.

I took the elevator up, and ran to Rhea's door, and knocked.

She opened her door, but when she saw it was me, she tried to close it. I forced my foot inside and pushed the door wide open.

Get out! she said and ran to the kitchen. Get out, she shouted. Out!

I could see that she had a black eye. Her hair was a mess, and she was clearly tired.

Who is the man from last night? I asked her.

Get out, she repeated and opened a kitchen drawer, plunged her hands inside, frantically scraped metal on metal, then pulled out a knife and brandished it at me. I told you not to follow me and not to interfere in my life.

I approached her, and she slowly retreated. I grabbed her by the wrist and pulled the knife from her hand. Then I dragged her back to the living room. I threw her on the sofa and said, I know that George would want me to protect you, and I will do so as long as I am here.

George! she screamed. George does not even know of my existence. I am free, do you understand? You do not interfere with my life! I will tell the police about you, and send you back to George and wherever you came from! She waved her hands at me. Then she took a deep breath, her hands fell, her voice softened, and she said, Leave. Please leave. You are causing me trouble. She gently pushed me.

Who is he? What is his full name? I said.

Vas te faire foutre, she said.

No one hits George's sister, and no one pulls a knife on either of us. I will find your Moshe, I said and walked out the door.

Yes, go! she said, following me. And take this with you. She threw an envelope at my back. Leave, and mind your own business. *Collant de merde!*

I picked up the envelope and ran back down the stairs. The envelope contained a ticket to Canada. The flight was in six days.

I walked slowly back to my hotel, and when I arrived, I called my generals and told them, We need to find the man from last night, and lay a plan.

At the hotel, I sent an officer to interrogate the man at the desk, to ask him if he had the information on the plate number. He came back with a negative answer. My officers and I paced and smoked pipes. Some of my officers had their feet on the table, showing their boots. The campaign room was filled with smoke, and maps on the table that detailed flowing rivers, mountains, and long plains.

We should attack soon, before your voyage to the new continent, comrade, one general with a droopy white moustache declared.

I agreed. We decided to dismiss the meeting and to each go on our own way and wait to hear of the enemy's whereabouts.

For two days I sent my officer to ask the man at the front desk about the licence-plate number, and always the answer was the same: He was working on it. Finally, on the third day, a messenger on a horse entered the military complex, breathing heavily. We have it, he said.

I opened the letter. The car was registered under Mani and Associates, Jules Favre, 52 rue de la Commune.

I called the revolutionaries. We met and decided on an attack plan.

I went to the address in the letter and watched the place. Eventually I saw the man I was waiting for, driving the same car as before. He parked his vehicle in the lot and went inside the building. I waited for a little while and then entered the building and watched from the bottom of a set of spiral stairs as his leather jacket ascended toward the heavens.

I went back home and consulted with my fellow fighters. All night we stayed awake, preparing for the attack. In the afternoon of the next day, I went down to the basement of my hotel. I opened the garbage bin and looked inside. Then I walked around the basement, searching, until I found a metal pipe lying on the floor between a pile of old chairs, a broken table, and an old sink.

I grabbed the pipe, pushed it inside my sleeve, and took the stairs back to my room.

I called my lieutenant and informed him that the ammunition had arrived.

He brought the horses, and that evening we rode to the enemy's territory. Our enemy's car was now parked down the street. I went over to it and started to rock it, until the car alarm went off. Then I pulled on my hat, rushed over to the stairs of the apartment building, hid between two floors, and waited for a door to open.

In the dim moonlight, I watched a man's silhouette rushing down the stairs. When he faced me, I lowered my hat over my eyes and said, *Bonsoir*, in a muffled voice. As soon as he passed by me, I hit him from behind. And before he had the chance to recover, I rushed toward him and gave him many blows from the whistling pipe in my hand. I frisked his pockets, pulled out his wallet, and picked up his car keys from the floor. Then I rushed down the stairs, jumped on my horse, and we galloped across the Parisian cobblestones while, in the background, we heard the car alarm lamenting in sorrow and pain.

That night, I had a series of nightmares. In one of them I saw myself drowning in a large sea that had shrunk to the shape of a tub. I dreamt of Roland pouring wine for me, and then, when he turned around from the sizzling stove, I saw Rambo's face telling me, *Ya habbub, we will send you back home.* As I ran down the stairs in my dream, George appeared to me, smiling and with a gun in his hand. He stood on the stairs, and leaned against the wall, and spun the barrel of his gun.

I woke up in a sweat; it took me a few minutes to realize that I was in Paris. I rushed to the door of my room and checked that it was locked. Then I locked the bathroom door. I sat at the window and gazed out at the darkness, and made sure that Paris was still Paris.

Still, flashbacks came to me rapidly, and I could not sleep. I thought of George, and I expected Rambo to come to my room and ask me to take a walk. I called myself a coward and many other names for fearing the ghost of that dead brute. *The dead do not come back*, I chanted and chanted.

I cursed Roland for asking me to throw away my gun. I blamed everything on my gun's absence. I did not have those dreams when my gun slept under my pillow, I thought to myself.

I paced my room. I chain-smoked, because in the underground torture dungeon, a lit cigarette was the thing I had most longed for.

I remembered how, when Rambo had held my neck and filled my nostrils with cold water, I had wondered about underwater smoking. And I remembered how my mother had smoked while thieving water from the neighbours' reservoir. As a kid, I had watched her climbing the thick pipes to reach the water tank. It had mesmerized me to see her plunging her entire upper body, including the cigarette on her lips, into the metal tank, and resurfacing with the cigarette still lit on her lips and a bucket filled with water in her hand. I had watched her before every dive, stretching her toes like a ballerina, exposing her thighs above my small figure while she fished for water, and like a sailor muttered curses (that echoed inside the water tank) of her life of sacrifice and her marriage to that good-for-nothing gambler father of mine.

And years later, I, like my mother, dived into that tub, under my torturer's supervision; I plunged my upper body, thinking of my mother's intact cigarette, of the Phoenix brand that never ceased to burn and never ceased to die. And when Rambo whispered to me, assuring me of my nearing death, I was relieved at my parents' absence, for my death like all death should be a death and an end – no memory, no photograph, no stories, and no mother's tears. In death, every-thing should cease. All else is nothing but human vanity and make-believe.

The next morning, cars passed by and honked, and the flags of a football team split the winds and trembled above cars, and people danced in the streets, drank and chanted aloud. When I opened the window, the noise rose; when I closed the window, the noise settled like the bedsheets that the hotel cleaning lady had flipped over my bed the day before while I sat in her presence and watched the sheets fall slowly, gracefully, like the flight of the partridge above sunny waters.

I had watched the cleaning lady disappear into the bathroom, tossing the towels in the bin, ignoring me, perhaps feeling my lusty looks at her short skirt, or my eyes untying her white apron. I had thanked her for every cup she changed, every paper she picked up, for every bend, for every sweep, every pillow cover she caressed, every quilt she tucked. When I offered her cigarettes, she smiled and said that she did not smoke. She took my ashtray and emptied it in a bag. I had asked her name. I had asked where she came from. And when I held her hand and shouted, Linda from Portugal, I will wait for you to come to my room every day! Let me caress your breast, let me fall gently upon you, she had pulled her hand back and rushed quickly out of the room, pushing her cleaning cart toward the freight elevator, sticking her head through the doors as they shut, making sure I did not follow her and hold her waist, and offer her money, and breathe in her ear, and push the elevator's stop button, and untie her white apron.

After that, an older man came to clean my room. He pushed the same cart and gave me a look that said, I know you, I know your type, the type who feeds on kitchen maids, single hard-working mothers, illegal workers, and silent cleaning ladies. He didn't greet me, and he treated me with disdain, turning the soft flight of the white sheets into suicidal falls, plane crashes, depriving me of the soft landings that I so longed for from Linda's hands.

Where is Linda? I asked him.

He spoke to me with hostility, in French with a heavy Portuguese accent. You stay away from my niece, you understand! he said, spitting on the carpet and flinging the door closed behind him.

That day, I received an invitation from Rhea. Please come and see me, she said. It is important.

I walked to her house. She opened the door, not looking at me, not saying a word. I sat at her window; she chose to sit in the chair farthest away from me.

The French embassy in Lebanon just got in touch with us, she said. We have been trying to get George a passport, but they have not been able to find him. They sent people to his house; they asked about him. They even got in touch with someone in the militia. No one knows his whereabouts. They checked the hospitals, the morgues – nothing. But you know something, don't you? Yes, you know something; I feel there are things you are not telling me. What do you think happened to him? I hate your silence. Look at your eyes! You do not even look me in the eyes. You do not even care, do you? You do not care. Talk to me, she said. Talk.

I stood up to leave. She shouted, Please, tell me. Please.

I kept silent and walked out of her house.

Bassam! Dis-moi, Bassam. Dis-moi quelque chose, putain, she shouted after me.

I walked toward the river. I sat on a bench and looked at the passing water and the returning clouds. Then I made a decision. I stood up and walked back to Rhea's place.

I buzzed the doorbell, but Rhea did not answer. I went across the street and called her name, but she did not answer. I waited, and ten thousand cars passed, and I watched and inhaled their fumes until one of them stopped on the street. I recognized Roland sitting inside it, along with the man I had beat with the pipe. I walked back behind a wall and watched Roland get out of the car. He leaned through the window; the two exchanged a few words. The man in the car nodded like an employee, and Roland walked away and buzzed Rhea's bell.

Now I waited on the streets of Paris with the impatience of a hungry lion for night to come. It rained, and still I waited and watched every fading light, every single ray that left and disappeared to the other side of the earth. And when night ascended from beneath the rivers, I rushed to the bridge where I had thrown away my gun. I saw a small fire flickering and a couple of old men around it, nursing a bottle of wine with their miserable palms and their toothless lips. I walked straight to the rope I had left there, and pulled it, but a weight held the gun from coming back to me. I fought the ten thousand devils who held on to the other side of the rope. Like the steady motion of the waves, they all counted to three and pulled away from me at the same time. I wrapped the rope around my arm and pulled it back toward me with all my strength, but the devils mocked me with their hairy, hunched backs, their featherless wings, their thick, meek, spiteful chanting voices. They rejoiced as they watched me clinging to the river stones and the metal beams, shifting from side to side and hovering above the unlit waters.

I walked into the river, and my feet plunged into the reflection of the old men's fire that danced on its surface. I waded into the river and pulled the rope from under the weight of sand and wicked litter. I advanced toward the ten thousand creatures underneath the banks of the river, and the water magnified my feet and made me seem like a giant warrior on a fearless path to hell. Slowly, I liberated the rope from the weight of open cans that clinked like metal crosses, and chased the demons away. I plunged beneath the water, and the men behind me watched me sink. They shouted and called me back; they asked me to change my mind and not to listen to the current and its diabolic sirens.

But I, with my bare hands, dug into the soil beneath the river and pulled out the bundle of nylon, and I felt the weight of my gun again. I held it under my arm. I rushed to the edge of the polished stones, and I scrubbed the rope around the nylon until it broke, and my gun was freed.

I walked above the wet streets and into the city gates with an arm in my hand.

CHAPTER 21

There was water underneath me, and water within me, and water from above me fell from the clouds.

I covered my gun with my jacket and walked back to my hotel. Before the concierge had a chance to squeeze out a comment about my wetness, I took the stairs to my room. I pushed a chair against the door. I took off the dead man's clothes I had been wearing and left them dripping on a chair. Then I took a warm shower, put on my old clothes, stole the soap in the bathroom, packed my belongings, and slipped down the stairs to the basement and out of the hotel through the kitchen to the little alley outside.

The rain had stopped.

All night, I rode the trains to nowhere. I watched doors open and close, swallowing humans, moving them from one place to another. I sat in the corner of the train, just as George always had. Always sit with your back to the wall, he used to say, and let your gun hang loose.

After midnight, the trains stopped, and I got off nowhere. I contemplated staying at the station, but there were police officers on a regular beat there. So I walked, and when I got tired, I sat in back alleys behind restaurant doors. I smoked and counted the little drops of rain that tumbled through the walls and whirled against the city's lamps.

In the morning, I called my hotel. I had decided to give Linda her tip and apologize for my devouring, lusty looks, and for chasing her with my eyes. Is Linda working today? I asked.

Linda?

Yes, the cleaning girl.

The voice paused, then said, No, it is her uncle's turn today.

What time does he finish work?

At noon.

At noon, I waited on the street outside the hotel.

When I saw the old man, I followed him. He had a bag under his arm and walked with his head down, close to the walls, counting cobblestones.

I followed him, and from behind, I shouted, Señor! Señor!

The old man turned and stopped. He did not recognize me.

I said, Señor, I am the man in room 201.

He turned and walked away. I trotted beside him like a dog, dipping my head and searching for his eyes.

Señor, I want to talk to you.

He was silent.

Señor, I just wanted to tell you that I regret what I said to Linda.

Now he stopped, looked me in the eye, and said, You people think that you can take advantage of poor working girls.

No, señor. I have respect, señor.

Respect. He paused, then said, She was afraid. She has to see men like you all the time. This old man, the night before, was playing with his thing. He knew she would enter, so when she knocked at the door, he did not answer. She is a good girl, and you people . . . He said something I could not understand in Portuguese and walked away.

Señor, I said. Please give Linda my regards, my respects. Tell her I am sorry and that she is a beautiful girl.

No.

Please, señor! I said and trotted beside him some more.

Young man, you come to this country, and you do nothing. I left Portugal at your age. I took Linda after her father was killed by Salazar. I worked to raise my niece and she is a good girl. You are not worthy of her hair! He waved his hands in the air around his chest.

Yes, señor. Yes, I am. I am worthy.

No, you are a man in trouble.

Why do you say that, señor?

The police came yesterday to the hotel and searched your room.

Police?

Yes, two policemen.

Are you sure they were police, señor?

Go away now, stop following me, he said.

Did one of them have a bandage, señor?

Go away.

Did he have a bandage on his head? Please, señor, tell me.

Yes! Now go away.

Señor, thank you, and tell Linda that I will always remember the way she flips the bedsheets, and her round, beautiful eyes. Tell her that I will wear black that matches her long lashes.

Conyo, he cursed me, with his fist in the air, and he walked on, counting the cobblestones, mumbling to the walls, descending to the trains, and cursing, echoing, spitting at the ground.

I called Rhea.

Do not call me any more, she said. Or maybe call when you are ready to tell me something worthy. I am tired of your clinging and your secrets.

I have a meeting with Roland at his house before I get on that plane to Canada, but I lost his address, I lied.

35 rue Fouchons, she said. She hung up immediately.

I took the train, and then walked to Roland's place. From across the Street I watched the entrance to his house. Soon, I saw the man I had beaten with the pipe, driving his big car. I waited until he dropped Roland off and left, and then I rushed to the door and entered the house behind Roland. I pulled out my gun and stuck in near his liver.

Let's have some tea, I said.

Roland slowly turned, and when he saw me he smiled.

Ah, *te voilà*. We were looking for you last night. We wondered if you would be leaving today.

I know. That is why I came.

Roland took off his gloves and his coat. No need for the gun. Come sit down, he calmly said to me. He went into his living room and sat.

I took a chair in the corner and let my gun hang loose in my hand.

You are a stupid idiot, he said to me. Listen, I will give you one more chance, and it is your last chance, he said. Put that gun down.

I lifted it and pointed it at his face. I am the one who should be giving chances here, I said.

Fine. He nodded.

The man with the bandage works for you, I said.

Moshe, you mean? Yes, he does.

Did you ask him to beat up Rhea? I said.

It is touching that you care. Sit down and do not be a stupid romantic.

Why did you beat her? I asked.

Because she is mine. Rhea has always been mine, since she was fifteen. Do you understand? Rhea's father worked for us. After his death, I took care

294

of her. The mother is a shopaholic, an empty society lady. Rhea was a neglected woman. Listen, my little boy, you are stepping into dangerous zones. But the good news is that we need something from you.

I have nothing to offer you, I said.

We need you to tell us what happened to George.

Why should you care about George?

George worked for us.

Us?

Yes, the Mossad. Us. We recruited him on his trip to Israel. George knows all about his father. We suspected that Abou-Nahra was opening up to the Syrians. He will probably get even closer to them – especially now, after the assassination of Al-Rayess. Al-Rayess was our man in the region. We armed his militia, trained them, and gave them strategies. You see, George kept track of him, he got close to him. And Abou-Nahra trusted him.

George was an agent?

Yes. A smart and a good one. So should you be, my boy, a smart and a good one. You tell us where George is. We know that the last time he was seen, he had volunteered to pick you up from your home. He wanted to ask you a few questions about your involvement with the Al-Rayess assassination. We know. We have agents with those Christians. All we have to do is ask. Talking to us is your only hope. You cannot go anywhere without our consent. Do you understand?

How much does Rhea know about this?

Only a little, Roland said. Only that we want you to tell us more about George.

What about the visa to Canada?

You would have been stopped at the airport in Paris, put in jail for fraud . . . And we would have intervened, giving you the option of release and a good lawyer if you told us what really happened to George. You would be in jail. What better place to keep you locked up than in a legitimate jail? And if you did not speak, we would have sent you a nice, big, loving guy to be your friend, if you know what I mean. You are small in this game, very small, Roland said. I will give you a few minutes to think. You lay the gun down on the coffee table if you want to talk. We can do something for you, maybe; if you do not talk, you will not go anywhere, believe me.

I stood up, pointed the gun in his face, and said, Put your hands on your head.

He did.

I frisked him and grabbed his wallet and sunglasses. There were a few hundred francs in the wallet. I took them.

On the floor, I ordered.

My men will be here in a minute, Roland said. I am giving you a last chance.

Do not move or I will shoot you, I said.

You are a petty thief! You are *un idiot*, he shouted from the carpet.

I stomped on the sunglasses and broke them. Then I rushed to the phone on a nearby table and pulled the wire from the jack. I tied Roland's hands with the wire, and took the house keys from his pocket. I walked toward the door and opened it slowly. When I saw nothing, I closed the door behind me and locked it. I ran down the stairs and into the streets, then through the back alleys toward Rhea's apartment.

When I reached Rhea's place, I called her from a phone booth across the street.

Didn't I tell you not to call me again? she said. And anyhow, don't you have a plane to catch?

I want to tell you about George now, I said.

She was silent for a moment. Then she said, Tell me.

It is not good, I said. The news is not good. I am across the street. Open your door to me.

When she agreed, I took the stairs up. I did not want to wait for the metal elevator to lift my thumping heart.

Rhea opened the door in tears. She held on to me briefly, and then, as if realizing that she was in the arms of the messenger of death, she pushed herself back and held her hand over her mouth.

So you've known all long what happened to George, she said.

The last time I saw George, it was just before I left, I told her.

She waved her hand to invite me into her home. When I entered, she turned her back to me, sobbing. I laid my hand on her back, but she shook her head. I held her shoulders and turned her gently toward me. She was still crying, and her tears spilled down her face.

George was my brother, I said.

I took a deep breath, then spoke without stopping. Once, George and I took our hunting guns and entered the high mountains, I began. We stood still like snakes, holding erect barrels and venomous powder. We stood still and watched for branches bowing under the weight of a feather, bowing to a mating call. And soon we wounded a little bird. I held it in my hand.

Kill it if it is still alive, George told me. Kill it!

But I couldn't bring myself to kill that little bird. Its beak opened and closed in silence, as if it was asking me for water. Its eyes began to close above my palm.

Kill it! Why are you looking at that wounded bird? Kill it and release it from its suffering. Finish it off. Your brother sounded irritated.

But I waited for the bird to fly again.

George snatched the wounded creature from my open palm. He laid it on a rock, and with the butt of his rifle he hit it on the head, more than once, and then he walked away, looking for more.

Why are you telling me this story? Rhea asked.

George and I killed more than birds, I told her.

People?

Yes, I said, and I told her about killing Khalil, and about our money scams, and our silent quarrels, and about George joining the militia. I told her all about Monsieur Laurent, and Nicole, and my torture.

Rhea listened, leaning her body against the sink, at times looking me straight in the eye, and at other times looking at the floor or the ceiling. Then she said, So, you are telling me all this, but where is George now?

I did not answer her directly. Instead, I continued talking about the massacre at the camp. I described to her what George had told me about the lights, the dog, the birds, the cadavers that piled up and rotted, the axes, the rivers of blood.

I talked and Rhea shook her head. Finally, she interrupted me, shouting, Okay, that is enough now. I don't know . . . I don't know why you have to come here now and tell me all this. She shook her head again. And you waited all this time to talk to me. Do you think it is a game? You waited, and where is my brother now? You tell me all these things, things that I do not know are even true. We don't know you. I don't know who you are. And yet you come and tell me all these evil things.

I ignored her shouting. I ignored her small eyes, and her twitching cheeks, her brown dress. I ignored her protest, and when she tried to leave the room, I held her back, cornered her against the kitchen sink. I told her about the night her brother took me under the bridge.

This is all confusing, Rhea said. Your stories are not making sense. I do not know these people you are talking about. You come here like this, and expect me to listen to it all. I need to leave, she said. Please let me go.

But I was merciless.

We sat in the car, under the bridge, I said to her. George and I quarrelled. He had come to take me to the militia headquarters just before I was leaving Lebanon. He picked me up in his car. I didn't want to go with him, but he kissed me, he called me his brother. He made me hop in his car, and we drove below the Nabaa Bridge. Your brother was sent to take me back to my torturer, and then they would have killed me. But he said that he would give me a chance. He played with his gun. He filled it with three bullets and spun it. He smiled, and then he said to me, I am giving you a chance.

I took the gun from his hand, and without blinking, without giving myself the time to think about the sea, the ship, the new place that I wanted so much to go to, I held the gun against my head and pulled the trigger. It clicked, and it did not go off.

I laid the gun next to me on the car seat. Your brother smiled. He picked up the gun slowly. He was not scared; no, he was composed, and as fearless as ever. He held the gun in his hand. Then he turned his face toward me, gave me a smile, and a shot went off.

Rhea held her hand to her mouth and struggled to leave my embrace. You knew all this, she said. You knew. And you . . .

I pushed her back, and said, I buried him there. I buried him under the bridge. The gun dropped on my feet, and George collapsed on me. There was an open wound. I could see the other side of his face, open, a piece of his brain hanging. The windshield turned red. And the red liquid moved down the glass and rushed toward the dashboard like rain. I sat and I watched the houses, the passing cars, submerging slowly in red rain. De Niro's hair spilled on my lap. I caressed it. I caressed it.

Without thinking, I touched Rhea's hair. She froze, scared.

I held her firmly by the shoulders and continued: I buried him under the bridge. I dragged him above the sewage, toward a pile of stones. I laid him next to it. I picked up the first large rock I saw, and put it against his head. Then I laid another rock on the other side. I surrounded him with stones, and then I went back to the car, took his gun and his rifle, and laid them at his side. I covered him with rocks and stones. And then I grabbed the sand, scooping it with my palms, to fill the space between the stones. He is there. Your brother is there, under that bridge.

You want to know his whereabouts? Listen, I said to Rhea. Listen. I went back to the car. I sat in the driver's seat. The windshield was drenched with blood. I tried to wipe it with my hand, but it just made it more opaque, somehow thicker, with large, wide lines. The blood was drying fast, and turning darker. Blood sticks. So I went back to that pile of sand, scooped up some more, and tried to rub it against the glass. Now everything turned to red mud, like that mythical river in our land. I just wanted to see the road, you see. I just wanted to see something else besides that doomed city. I just wanted to leave.

Rhea looked me in the eye then, and slightly twisted her shoulder, but I dropped my hands onto hers and said quietly, Please let me finish.

She barely nodded, and I could feel her body sagging with weakness, her knees bending and almost touching mine.

I broke that car's glass, I said. I went back and chose the largest rock I could carry. I laid it on the car's hood. I went back inside the car, pulled a jacket from my bag, and put it on the driver's seat. I climbed out of the car and up onto the hood. And I lifted the rock, and smashed it against the windshield. The glass broke in a million little pieces.

I lifted my jacket from the driver's seat and flung it against the sky, and got rid of all the little stones. I was surrounded by ten thousand glowing red-and-green diamonds. I laughed. After that, I drove away fast, and the wind was in my eyes. I drove, and the wind rushed through my shirt, and tears fell from my eyes, but I was not crying. The wind hit my face, and it felt as if my head was pushed under water again. I gasped for little breaths, exhaling the smell of blood. And then the blood got thicker on my hands. I couldn't hide it; it was in front of my eyes. And it took over the wheels and the car, and it started to move through the lanes, fast, passing cars and diesel trucks. The blood on my hands was swinging the car out of control. So I had to get rid of the blood.

I drove the car onto a small dusty road, and I drove through a green meadow that led me to the sea. I left the car and rushed to the rocky shore, and I stepped into the water, and started to clean myself of my sins, of this burning land, of my loved ones. And the sea turned purple, like the onyx that had once filled the shore. And the blood screamed louder than the seagulls, louder than the ancient invaders. I buried my head in the waves and washed my hair. The pebbles behind me rocked back and forth; the clams shut their shells. I sat between land and sea, vomiting what I did not eat, spitting out the yellow substance that joined the sea foam and rushed past me to shatter on the massive rocks.

After a while, I went back to the car and stripped myself of the clothes I was wearing. I opened my bag and put on the other clothes that I had packed.

Then I drove away from there, and I did not think of George. You see? You see? All I wanted was to ride away on the sea.

I pulled back from Rhea. I had nothing more to say.

She didn't turn away from me then, but still I left her in tears. I went down her stairs and into Paris's streets.

I walked to the train station. It rained, and the trains arrived and departed, and the passengers passed.

The woman at the ticket window asked me, *Monsieur, où allez-vous aujourd'hui?*

Roma, I said. Roma.

GLOSSARY OF ARABIC TERMS

AKHU AL-SHARMUTA: brother of a bitch

ALA ALAARD YA IKHWAT AL-SHARMUTA: Down on the floor, you brothers of bitches

AL-AMN AL-DAKHILI: internal security

AL-ASWAQ: marketplace; a reference to the region that divided East from West Beirut during the Lebanese civil war

AL-GHARBIYYAH: West Beirut

ALLAH YIRHAMHA: may she rest in peace

AL-NASIK: the Hermit

ARAQ: distilled alcohol made of grapes

ARBA'IN TWAKKAL ALA ALLAH: Forty, God be with you

ARGILAHS: hookahs

ARS: pimp

ASAS: foundation

BATAL: hero

BAMIA: okra

BONSOIRAYN: Lebanese slang meaning *bonsoir* twice

CHABBAB: young men

DABKAH: a group circular dance

DANTA, YA BEH, MUSH AYIZ IDDIK CRAVATA HARIR

KAMAN?: Your highness, do you want me to offer you a silk tie as well?

FANNAS: a liar

GEORGE AL-FARANSAWI: George the French

HABIBTI: my darling

HAMSHAH, SHALKHAH: slang meaning hot, attractive girl

HASHASH: drug user

HAYDI AL-SARSARAH: this gossiper

IRAN: a liquid yoghurt

JABHAH: the name of a place, or a faction, on the front line

JAHILIYYAH: pre-islamic period

KALASH: slang for Kalashnikov, a weapon used widely in the war

KANASA: snipers

KASS: a drink based on green almonds

KAYF: joy; slang for hashish

KHALAS: enough, or finish

KHALL: vinegar

KUNAFAH: a cheese pie

LABNAH: soft cheese

LAHM BA'AJIN: a thin meat pie

MAJALIS: the name of the headquarters of the Lebanese Forces

MAJNUN: crazy

MAN'oushe: thyme pie

MARIAM AL-ADHRA': Virgin Mary

MASHKAL: problem

MASSAT: blowjobs

MAZAH: an assortment of finger foods

MUQAWAMAH: resistance

RAKWAH: a small pot with a short spout used to make Arabic coffee

RJA' YA ALLAH-RJA'!: Go back, for God's sake

RUH: spirit

RUMMANAH: pomegranate; slang for a hand grenade

SAHTAYN: good appetite

SAKANAH: an army barricade

SHABAB: young men

SHAHID: martyr

TANTE: aunt

TWAKKALALA ALLAH: Have faith in God

'UMMAH: nation

'USTADH: teacher

WOU YALLAH SHID YA BEEBO SHID MITL MA SHAD BAYAK AWWAL LAYLAH: Push, push Beebo, in the same way your father pushed on his wedding night

YA CHIC INTA: handsome

YA HABBUB: a term of endearment

YA IKHWAT AL-SHARMUTA: brothers of bitches

YA KALB: dog

YA KHALTI: my aunty

YA 'UM AL-NUR: Mother of Light

YA WLAD AL-sharmuta: sons of bitches

YALLAH, KASSAK: cheers

YASSAREH: leftist

ZAJAL: a form of improvised dialect poetry

ZAKHIRAH: a piece of wood the Lebanese Christians believe originated from Jesus' cross

ZU'RAN: thugs

ACKNOWLEDGEMENTS

I would like to thank the Canada Council and the Conseil des arts et des lettres du Québec for their support. I also would like to thank Lisa Mills for her presence, friendship, and support during the writing of this book and after. Thanks to John Asfour for his friendship and much-appreciated guidance. To my publisher Lynn Henry, and all the people at Anansi, and to Martha Sharpe for acquiring the manuscript and for ongoing support. Thanks to my brothers and family: Mark, Merdad, Ralph, Gigi, and Ramzi. A special thanks to: Dima Ayoub, Leila Bdeir, Laurence Cailbeaux and Jesh Hanspal, Nick Chbat, Tina Diab, Jocelyn Doray, Julia Dover, Eva Elias, Majdi El-Omari, Erin George, Kathryn Haddad, Mansour Harik, Nasrin Himada and Raphaelle Beaulieu, Magdalona Gombos, Aida Kaouk, Sandra Khoury, Johanna Manley, Ramzi Moufarej, Nehal Nassif, Maire Noonan and Antoine Boustros, Milosz Rowicki, Babak Salari, Julian Samuels, Pascale Solon, Laurelle Sprengelmeyer, and Shannon Walsh.

Any resemblance of characters in this novel to persons living or dead is purely coincidental.